Pride Publishing books by Kristian Parker

Speak Its Name
To Light a Fire
Call it Love
Spotlight on Love

Village Affairs
The Rule of Three
Three's Company
Triple Intent

Two Tribes
Fool's Gold
Everything Changes
Don't Look Back in Anger

Collections
My Bloody Valentine: Venetian Valentine
Sun, Sea and Spotted Squid

I0607629

Two Tribes

DON'T LOOK BACK IN ANGER

KRISTIAN PARKER

Don't Look Back in Anger
ISBN # 978-1-80250-543-6
©Copyright Kristian Parker 2023
Cover Art by Erin Dameron-Hill ©Copyright May 2023
Interior text design by Claire Siemaszkiewicz
Pride Publishing

DON'T LOOK
BACK IN ANGER

Dedication

To P.B. May your crisps be flavoursome and your ale floweth freely! Thank you for all the laughs. I don't know what I'd do without them.

Chapter One

Lorenzo de Luca turned off the motorway into the suburbs of South Manchester. Back in the day, he'd had a little bedsit around here. It had been fifteen years since he'd been here. Surely they hadn't changed the roads, though.

A building that used to house a tailor's and now held a vape shop told him he had the right street. As he drove up, his heart sank. The little row of terraced houses that had been converted into bedsits was long gone. A soulless red-brick block sat in its place with a ton of cars outside. He supposed this was progress.

To be fair, the bedsit had been pretty ropey. One of the windows never fully shut and the neighbour used to play music at all hours of the day and night. Lorenzo hadn't cared. He had been in his twenties and loving that he had a place to call his own. But he wouldn't be seen dead having a coffee in a place like that these days, never mind staying the night. He had come a long way since those days.

His old home hadn't been his main destination anyway. He parked up and walked in the footsteps of his twenty-seven-year-old self.

Many a time, he, Jonny and Harry had staggered up this street after spending some of their ill-gotten gains in the bars nearby. They'd been untouchable in those days—Lorenzo and Harry had helped Jonny take control of Manchester's criminal underworld. Everyone cowered when Jonny Wellingham's Boys swaggered past—their reputation for swift justice had been earned tenfold.

Lorenzo crossed the road and soon found the path he wanted. It ran up a back alley of the next street. The red brick walls of the terraces hadn't changed. Memories flooded into his mind like a tsunami.

At the end of the alley, he came to a big car park where he and the lads would set up shop every Wednesday. A regular community operation trading out of a clapped-out Volkswagen campervan. The police had never known a thing.

At the weekends, they'd only dealt in town. However, Jonny had soon realised that a lot of people liked to have their drugs before a night out. So, he would arrange for the van to be in this out-of-the-way spot and punters would come under cover of darkness to do their shopping. One man exclaimed they could only do better if they had a reward points system.

For a moment, Jonny had actually considered it.

A number of public pathways led off the car park. They followed a network of man-made waterways that had been dug to save the area from flooding. As a by-product, they had also created a thriving nature reserve. City dwellers, starved of green space, used them for cycling, jogging and dog walking.

The area had been gentrified since Lorenzo's day. When he had been here, these walkways were the domain of alcoholics and working girls whose customers didn't mind a bunk up against a tree. It was hilarious to him that the middle classes now brought their kids here to study wildlife.

Lorenzo hadn't come here to see insects or birds today. He could remember running through the car park as though the devil himself were after him. Tracing his previous footsteps, knowing what had awaited him that night, sent chills across his skin.

There had been few times in his life when he had experienced real terror. That night, fifteen years ago, still haunted his nightmares.

He'd been watching television in his little flat when they'd burst through the door. Two of them had grabbed his arms while Frank, one of Jonny's lads, had walked up to him.

Lorenzo and Frank had always got on well. The distress at why they had come to inflict pain on him burnt as hot today as it had then. That was before Lorenzo had learnt that true loyalty was a rare diamond, to be cherished when found.

"Wellingham doesn't like your sort," Frank had sneered, grabbing his face. "Shirt-lifters. Problem for you is, he can't just sack you. That leaves only one way out, Lorenzo."

A flash of metal told him all he needed to know about Frank's intentions. Before he could aim, Lorenzo had broken free and leapt through the downstairs window.

The scars on his calves still told that story. His legs had been burning with pain as he'd run across the tarmac, desperate to get to the darkened paths. His thinking had been that he knew this area well. He hoped his attackers didn't.

Retracing that fateful night, he followed the twists and turns. They seemed so innocent in the cold winter sunlight. He could still remember the taste of metallic dread in his mouth. In those days, Lorenzo had been fast. Yet his pursuers had fanned out so he didn't know which way to turn. Voices sounding from every angle sent him into a whirlpool of fear and confusion.

He rounded a hawthorn bush and stopped in his tracks. The hairs on the back of his neck stood on end. *The little pool where my flight came to an end.* The first bullet hit him like a juggernaut smashing into his shoulder. He'd lost his balance and fallen face down into the pool. The pain had seared through his body like hot knives. Instinctively, he reached up and touched where only a scar remained.

Two more bullets had hit him after that, one puncturing a lung. The other had narrowly missed any organs and gone straight through him. Doctors in his future would tell him how lucky he had been. Lying in that ice cold water, waiting to die, luck hadn't felt very close to him.

He'd silently prayed to God to take him quickly, yet he hadn't lost consciousness. Instead, he'd lain there, as still as possible, while his would-be assassins discussed if they'd killed him or not. Every second, he expected an insurance bullet to blow his brains out.

Then his hopes had soared when he'd thought they might be retreating. He'd barely been able to trust his ears as the sounds of his attackers faded.

Lorenzo crouched down and ran his hands through the water. The silt made it a dirty brown. He could imagine a time it would have been deep red with his blood.

Standing up, he filled his lungs with Manchester air. "I am back," he said out loud.

Seeing the place he'd lain, terrified to even breathe, brought a resolve to him. His body had almost frozen as he lay there, waiting to be sure they had gone. Once he could take no more, he had crawled out of the pool, the blood loss and cold making him limp and unable to get up. Instead, Lorenzo had crawled to the car park. Eventually he had got to the main road and thankfully someone driving past had seen him.

They'd saved his life, and he had no idea who they were. He wished he did. They had gone before the paramedics arrived. He supposed they'd recognised him and wanted nothing more to do with it. He could understand that. A man with three gunshot wounds screamed danger. He'd been lucky they'd even dared make the emergency call.

Today he planned to be the one to make an anonymous call. Adrenaline coursed through his veins as he got out the piece of paper with a number written on it. He'd got it from his nephew's friend. She'd thought he intended to use it to taunt Jonny. In a way he did, although he had a much more important outcome on his mind too.

With a shaking hand, he connected the call.

"Who is this?" came the voice that he hadn't heard in decades yet still seemed so familiar to him. "This is a private number. How did you get it?"

"It's a blast from your past," Lorenzo replied.

"Tell me who you are."

"Meet me at the location I message to you," Lorenzo continued. "And all will be revealed. Come alone if you want me to show myself."

He terminated the call. The fish was on the hook. Now he just had to reel it in.

* * * *

Nerves and excitement surged through his body like a runaway train. In every other part of his life, he held control with a tight fist. No one dared change his toilet detergent without checking with him first. He'd buried his feelings for so many years, opting for meaningless sex and making money. Now he had to face them. Lorenzo prided himself on his reputation of fearing no man. That wasn't the case today.

He walked to the exit of the car park and out onto a little square lined with restaurants and shops. It resembled a set from a sci-fi movie. A huge chrome building dominated the place. It housed a theatre and gallery. When he'd lived here, it had only just opened. Now it presided over an entire entertainment complex.

Salford Quays had certainly changed. The Manchester Ship Canal curled around the buildings full of TV channels and media outlets. What had once been the centre of industry now led the way in technology. He supposed Jonny Wellingham had lapped up all this new media money. They spent big and a lot of them on the product that Wellingham specialised in. He wouldn't take kindly to losing it. The thought made Lorenzo grin.

He strolled along the water's edge, pulling his collar up against the icy wind that blew over the water relentlessly. *I wonder what else has changed in*

Manchester? Ever since he'd arrived, he'd spent his time organising things at the farmhouse hideout his nephew, Marco, had set up. He hadn't had much of a chance to seek out his old haunts.

The other side of the theatre lay deserted. It only housed a goods entrance. There was a walkway with benches facing the water. Lorenzo clocked a CCTV camera on the building. It couldn't be more perfect. Quiet enough for privacy but no one would attempt anything here.

Leaning against the iron railing, he stared into the water.

What if he doesn't show?

Before he even thought about the consequences of that, he heard footsteps on the stone staircase he'd just come down. It had to be him.

"So, who the fuck are you then?"

Lorenzo turned, and there he stood. The man he had loved more than anyone in the whole world. The man he'd dreamt about and the man he'd almost been killed for. To have him standing in front of him was more than his heart knew what to do with.

A movie reel of memories spun through his mind at warp speed. So many times, he'd wanted to reach out and tell him everything. His thirst for revenge had always trumped his need for reconciliation.

"Hello, Harry," he said.

Harry frowned. "Do I know you?"

Lorenzo made a face. "I haven't aged that much in fifteen years, have I?"

Still Harry stared as though he'd never set eyes on him before. This moment reminded Lorenzo of being at the top of the rollercoaster. Chaos awaited and there wasn't any other option than to wait for it all to play out. Except these days, he drove the rollercoaster.

"Stop fucking me about," Harry said. "Either tell me who you are or I'm out of here."

Lorenzo walked a little closer. Harry instinctively gripped something in his pocket. Of course, he might have come alone, but he was clearly armed. Harry always had been the more paranoid of the two of them. Lorenzo had had a cockiness that drove a lot of people mad. That bravado had nearly cost him his life.

"Steady on," Lorenzo said. "I survived one shooting. I might not make it through another."

Realisation dawned on Harry's face. "What…it can't be."

Strolling over to him, Lorenzo stared him in the eye. "Take a good look. Surely you remember this face."

Poor Harry looked like he was about to pass out. He wobbled for a second and Lorenzo ran forward, grabbing him. "Do you need to sit down?" he asked.

Harry just nodded. His breathing came in little gasps for air and his legs shook violently. Lorenzo guided him over to a bench and sat him down. Harry put his head between his legs and for a minute or so, remained stock-still.

Did I overdo the drama? Imagine if I killed Harry before we've even had a chance to say hello.

"I'm sorry, I didn't know how else to tell you," Lorenzo said as calmly as he could manage. "I wanted you to see me, otherwise you might not believe it was me."

Eventually, Harry raised his head and just stared at him. "Can it be?"

Lorenzo nodded. "It's me, my love. Back from the dead and so fucking pleased to see you."

Chapter Two

"How?" he said. "How the fuck are you here? You're *dead*."

Chuckling, Lorenzo sat next to him on the bench. "Well, clearly I'm not." Lorenzo rested his hand on Harry's arm. "See, I'm not a ghost."

The connection, albeit through Harry's thick woollen coat, was the first they'd had since the last night they'd spent together. It felt like fire. Did Harry have the same reaction? He didn't pull his arm away.

"How?" Harry repeated.

Lorenzo stared out to the water. "Jonny's men shot and didn't check, the stupid bastards. I do hope he's tightened up his operation these days."

"But…"

Poor Harry didn't seem capable of forming coherent speech.

"They left me for dead," Lorenzo explained. "Luckily, someone found me and called the ambulance. I made it home after a very long stay in a Liverpool hospital."

Harry frowned. "Liverpool?"

"I must have been talking in my sleep. When the police heard Jonny Wellingham's name, they thought it best to move me," Lorenzo replied. "I don't remember much about it. I was otherwise engaged bleeding all over the place."

"Fuck," Harry said. "I can't take this in."

"The poor coppers thought they had a key witness to send old Jonny down for life," Lorenzo said with a chuckle. "I bet they were pissed when they found my empty bed."

"You weren't tempted?"

"Not in the slightest. When I take my revenge on that slimy piece of shit, he'll know it's come from me. I was in no shape. He fucked my body and my mind."

They sat in silence for a second. Lorenzo lit a cigarette and allowed Harry to process the last five minutes.

Harry suddenly whirled around on the bench. "Why didn't you get in touch? How could you let me think you were dead?"

Typical of Harry to dive straight in there once he's regained his composure. He was never one to mess about. He looked good. A few lines had appeared around his eyes, but they only served to give him an air of wisdom.

Lorenzo remembered the crazy, handsome guy he used to ride around the streets of Manchester with. When Jonny had gifted them a brand-new Mercedes, they had sung *Greased Lightnin'* at the tops of their voices. They had thought they ruled the world.

"I wanted to," he began. Harry's face suggested he didn't believe him. "Honestly, I did. When I got to Roma, things were bad. In here." He pointed to his head. "I wanted to close the door on everything that happened here."

Harry took the cigarette from Lorenzo's hand and had a long drag on it. "Until now."

"Until now," he agreed.

Reaching towards him, Harry turned Lorenzo's face so he could see him better. "I can't believe it. You're here. In front of me."

A tear escaped his eye. Lorenzo wiped it away. "I'm sorry to do it like this," he murmured. "You know I always liked a bit of theatre."

Harry snorted. "That's saying something. My God, I can't believe my eyes. Lorenzo de Luca. Still as handsome as ever."

Lorenzo grinned. "You too, my friend. A little thicker around the middle than I remember."

"Well, if we're playing that game, what's with all the grey hair?"

Running his hand through his thick grey curls, Lorenzo pouted. "Age comes to us all in the end. After what I've experienced in my life, I am nothing but grateful."

A pleasure boat sailed past. People were tucking into a meal and staring up at the theatre behind them. If they only had the slightest inkling of the drama being played out on a bench, right before their eyes. Plus, it was only a taster. Lorenzo had bigger plans than this for marking his return to the northern city where he had learnt so many lessons. Some of them good but most of them bad.

"I'm glad life came back to you," Harry said, quietly. "Even if I couldn't be around to share it."

They had dreamt of a whole different future back in the day, involving making as much money as possible and riding off into the sunset. He wondered what Harry had settled for after Lorenzo had gone missing. Liam, his nephew's lover, had told him a few stories. It appeared Harry still played second-in-command for Jonny. That didn't surprise him. Jonny could always tell when people were useful to him.

"We were crazy kids, were we?" Lorenzo said. "Do you remember that old Merc we had? I think we had about fifty places to stash pills. The coppers never stood a chance."

Harry's eyes filled with tears. "We were. God, it's good to see you. I don't know what to say."

The urge to lean forward and kiss Harry almost overwhelmed Lorenzo, but that wasn't the purpose of today's reunion. He needed to control himself.

"Why now?" Harry asked. "Why today?"

Lorenzo considered him for a second. "Are you asking for you or your boss?"

Jonny Wellingham might as well have been sitting on the bench with them, like a third guest who hadn't been invited. He would infect this reunion no matter what.

Conflict washed across Harry's face. "Both, I suppose."

"Refreshingly honest, Harry. You've not changed all that much." Lorenzo prepared himself to make a leap of faith that would prove to him whether Harry could still be trusted. Nerves jangled within him. "I want a meeting with him."

Harry exhaled. "You're fucking joking, aren't you? Things are kicking off at the moment. A new gang..." Realisation dawned on Harry's face. "It's *you*, isn't it?"

Lorenzo laughed. He risked really pissing Harry off, but why shouldn't he enjoy his little moment? "I believe you've met my nephew, Marco. Don't worry, I won't hold pulling his tooth out against you. It was just business, no?"

Harry clutched his head in his hands. "Jesus Christ, Lorenzo. What are you doing? Jonny will kill you all. He's fucking raging."

Lorenzo had taken the first proper step towards Jonny Wellingham's retribution. He understood Marco's frustrations at not being able to go in all guns blazing — this first taste whetted his appetite and he craved more. "It's payback time," he snarled. "He took everything and left me for dead. I want to make him suffer."

Harry scrubbed his face with his hand. Lorenzo almost pitied him.

"The killings at the farm is only the beginning. He wants your nephew's head on a stick. Liam's too," Harry whispered. "Lorenzo, please. You've made your point. Just go home to Italy before he gets wind of what's really happening."

"Where has he got this new gang from?" Lorenzo ignored Harry's pleas. "Tell me that at least."

Harry shook his head. "I can't tell you anything. You know how this works."

"Still loyal to the wrong man," Lorenzo muttered. "Haven't you learnt a thing?"

Anger flared across Harry's face. "Why are you here? With me, I mean? Why didn't you make your grand reveal to Jonny?"

A question that most people at the farm will want to know the answer to as well. "Two reasons. I want to see if I can trust you. Jonny will have his 'what the fuck' moment only if you keep your mouth closed. It's all up to you, Harry."

"And the other?"

"The other? Isn't it obvious? I wanted to see you in private. I didn't know how I would feel, did I?"

Harry seemed lost in thought for a second. Lorenzo's words hung in the air like unwanted Christmas decorations. "And how do you feel?" he asked.

"About the same as I did fifteen years ago. And I'll be honest, I didn't see that coming."

Harry leapt off the bench as if it were on fire. He went over to the railing, grabbing hold of it before facing Lorenzo. "Don't do that," he said. "It's so long ago, Lorenzo. I've moved on."

Lorenzo chuckled, throwing his practically unsmoked cigarette to the floor and getting up. He sauntered over to Harry, who had fear in his eyes. "That's not what Liam tells me. *'Lives alone. Never had a relationship. Still Jonny Wellingham's lapdog.'* That's pretty much how I left you, by my reckoning."

He hated how petty he sounded. His jealousy of Jonny having Harry all these years made him so angry.

"How is Liam?" Harry asked.

Lorenzo hadn't intended a change in conversation. Harry just casually asked about the boy after what he and Jonny had done to him. "He's fine," he replied. "No thanks to you and your boss. You killed his fucking mother and tried to kill him."

Harry held up his hand. "I had no idea about his mother. You can't put that on me. Don't you dare come here from God knows where and judge me. You've done worse and I'm sure this leopard doesn't change its spots. Have you bought yourself a new conscience?"

Harry's holier-than-thou attitude riled him. "Things are very different now. I have the cash and the muscle. I'm going to pay Jonny for the scars he left on my back."

"Then what?"

"Then I'll find out who told him about me and finish them as well. Someone tipped him off."

That had driven him mad all these years. Jonny had found out about his sexuality and dealt with him in the blink of an eye. It wasn't a gradual realisation. Someone had nearly cost him his life. Lorenzo would avenge that, tenfold.

"Is this really worth it?" Harry asked. "No one knows about this apart from me. Pack up and go. You must have a life in Italy."

Lorenzo hadn't expected Harry to welcome him with open arms. He had expected him to at least understand his motivation. "I'm disappointed in you, Harry. You can't even try to see it from my point of view?"

"I don't want any more unnecessary bloodshed," Harry replied. "I'm glad to see you, Lorenzo. Honestly, I am. To think you survived is more than I could ever have hoped for. What you're planning will be the end of all of us."

"Only one person. I will protect you, no matter what happens," Lorenzo promised.

They stood facing each other.

"I have something for you," Lorenzo said.

He produced a ring out of his pocket. Harry's eyes widened. "I gave you that," he said.

A thick gold ring that they had bought on a day trip. Jonny had landed a huge deal and given them all a decent pay packet. Lorenzo and Harry had gone to Edinburgh for a weekend. They'd told the others they were going to find girls. In reality, they'd barely left the hotel room.

One morning, they'd been walking around the shops and Harry had bought him a gold ring. It had a sovereign coin set in it where a jewel would sit. He'd vowed he would never take it off. For the last fifteen years, it had lived in his underwear drawer. Sometimes he would get it out just to stare at it and reminisce. For the most part it had stayed hidden. *Until now.*

"Keep it safe." Lorenzo placed it in Harry's jacket pocket. "I know this is a lot to take in. If you ever want to return it, I'll be waiting."

"I have to go," Harry replied.

He went to move. Lorenzo grabbed him by the arm. "Remember. This is your chance to prove if I can trust you. Tell Wellingham about me and I'll know you're lost. You have a choice, Harry."

Harry wrenched his arm free. "Don't serve me an ultimatum. Who the fuck do you think you are? I'll do as I please."

Lorenzo smiled. "And so will I."

Shaking his head, Harry gazed into his eyes. "What a fucking morning. It's good to see you. Even if you nearly gave me a heart attack."

Rummaging in his pocket, Lorenzo handed him a business card. "I want you to call me whenever you need me."

To his relief, Harry pocketed the card.

"Do I not even get a hug?" Lorenzo asked, throwing his arms wide.

Harry seemed to think about this before walking into his embrace. The familiar smell flooded Lorenzo's system and he drew him tight. "Oh, God, this feels good," he whispered in Harry's ear.

Harry broke away, wiping his eyes. "I can't do this. I'm sorry."

Lorenzo watched him go as he bolted up the steps. He desperately wanted him to stop and run down again.

Harry didn't look back once.

Chapter Three

Lorenzo drove into the farmyard. Marco had found this place and for some reason decided it would be ideal as their headquarters. In some respects, he had a point. After Marco's lover had been wounded by Wellingham, they'd needed to lie low. This farm had been perfect until Wellingham had found out where they were.

Lorenzo's nephew Giovanni and their friend Dolly had lost their lives for that mistake. Lorenzo blamed himself. He should have come sooner. He had only intended Marco to get a foothold in the Manchester market. Unfortunately, his nephew could be headstrong and had taken it upon himself to go for Jonny. Lorenzo allowed himself to feel a little pride. That was exactly what he would have done.

It had forced Lorenzo's hand, and he had arrived with an army behind him. Five campervans were parked in a row. One of the lads he had brought over from Italy gave him a wave.

"*Ciao, capo.*"

"Diego. What did I say? We speak English in England."

"Sorry, boss."

Lorenzo clocked the new CCTV cameras on every corner of the building. At least his orders had been carried out. The lads were all fairly new to his operation—he'd lost a good amount at a shootout in Naples. Luckily, they were quick learners. If only Marco was the same.

As Lorenzo walked into the kitchen, the smell from the oven stank the house out. He couldn't even work out what the hell it had started life as. His nephew Tommasso produced a dried-up joint of beef from the cooker, acrid smoke filling the kitchen.

"What the fuck is that?" Matteus, one of Lorenzo's boys, asked.

Tommasso banged it down on the top of the kitchen table. "I think I left it in too long," he groaned, rubbing his head. "I don't understand the bloody cooker. It's ancient."

"It's a shame Liam's brother has gone," Matteus replied. "At least he could make food we could actually eat."

Tommasso raced across the room and grabbed him by the shirt. "If you think you can do any better, try it with this knife up your arse."

Lorenzo banged on the table. "Enough. Tommasso. Put that knife down. Take my car and go and find somewhere that does fish and chips. You can't move for them. Matteus, you go with him, and play nicely, boys. I'm getting too old to referee childish squabbles."

Ignoring the grumbling from Tommasso, Lorenzo walked into the lounge. His nephew Marco and his boyfriend, Liam, were playing on a games console. His other two nephews Federico and Gabriel were fiddling with their phones as usual. Lorenzo missed conversation. A dying art, it appeared.

"Liam," Lorenzo said. All four men snapped to attention. "A word please."

They both went through to the little room that Lorenzo ironically called the office. Liam looked worried as he perched on the end of the desk. "Relax." Lorenzo lit a cigarette. "You're not in trouble. I want your advice."

Liam frowned. Lorenzo had a good feeling about this lad. He had been Jonny's lackey for too many years. According to Enzo, he and Marco made a great team. The loss of Giovanni and Dolly still smarted. The pair of them would have to prove their worth.

"You worked for that asshole Wellingham for ten years," he said. "What do you think his next move will be?"

Lorenzo smiled as the young lad screwed his face up as he tried to think. He had every intention that Marco would be his successor...if he could just calm himself down. Liam seemed to be the answer to this problem. Plus, his inside knowledge of Wellingham's gang could prove useful over the next few weeks. Lorenzo had every intention of diverting Liam's attention from Marco and towards the job in hand. He also had plans for Marco. Plans he would not like, but tough luck.

"He'll think he's the biggest cock on the walk," Liam said. "He'll be trading all over the place and telling everyone what a brave man he is. He'll also have everyone watching out for me and Marco. We're unfinished business for Jonny. He's got a whole new gang, although fuck knows where from. I guess there are always idiots like me willing to do whatever for the man with all the money."

"You're no idiot, Liam," Lorenzo said. "Have you noticed something about the gang I brought over from Italy? Think about it."

Liam shook his head. "I'm not sure what you're getting at."

"They are men. Not one of them is younger than twenty-three. When did you join Wellingham? When you were fifteen? Sixteen?"

Leaning against the windowsill, Liam frowned. "I was sixteen. I thought he was God's gift. I didn't fancy him or anything, but you know what I mean. He had it all, house, car, loads of cash. Who wouldn't be taken in by all that? Especially with the way me and Shaun were dragged up."

Jonny had always had that approach. He hated the idea that someone might be cleverer than him. The only person that had ever been exempt from that was Harry. Even in the early days, there had been a bond between Jonny and Harry. Lorenzo had often been jealous of it, even when he had Harry in his bed.

"Wellingham preys on boys like you were. He gets them to look up to him, then traps them," Lorenzo said. "That's not the de Luca style. My men are here because they want to be. They will serve me all the better for it."

Ever since he had made it home to Italy, injured and in shock, he had vowed he would run his mob differently. There had to be some honour, otherwise what was the point? His papa had instilled fairness in all of them. As the eldest boy, he took the responsibility of following in his father's footsteps very seriously.

"I don't care if he gets every kid on the block. I want you to make him pay," Liam said with fervour. "He deserves it for everything he has done."

"You'll get a ringside seat," Lorenzo replied. "That's if you want it."

Liam considered this for a second. "He killed my mother," he said finally with a face like stone. "I want it more than you could know."

Lorenzo nodded and clapped him on the shoulder. "You will have it. I promise."

At that moment, Marco came in. He glanced from one to the other. "Sorry, did I disturb something?"

"Not at all," Lorenzo said. "Did you want me?"

Marco glared from Lorenzo to Liam and back again. "No. I'd like to know what's going on."

Once again, Marco seemed to be under the control of his temper. Each time he reacted like this, it disappointed Lorenzo. It showed how much work they still had to do.

Lorenzo turned to Liam. "Can you give me and my nephew some time?"

Liam nodded. "Marco," he said as he walked past his lover. "Don't be a dick."

They waited for Liam to close the door behind him before Lorenzo gestured to the chair next to his. "Do we need to have a talk?"

Marco sighed and slumped down in the chair. Just like the stroppy little boy Lorenzo had adored. The act didn't transfer well to adulthood—If he intended on filling Lorenzo's shoes one day, he had a few hard lessons coming. "Marco," he said, "I won't have attitude from you. You know the situation."

Picking at the flaking varnish on the chair arm, Marco wouldn't meet his gaze.

"Marco. I'm talking to you."

Marco stopped and raised his face, a picture of defiance. Lorenzo would be fuming if he didn't see so much of himself in his nephew. "That makes a change," Marco said eventually. "You've been here nearly a week and you've barely spoken to me. Not about anything important."

"Things have been bedlam around here," Lorenzo replied. "We may be close, but I don't have to justify my actions. Please remember that."

"Well at least you've managed to bond with Liam. That's the main thing," Marco muttered, with a haughty expression that had begun to sorely test Lorenzo's patience. He would let his nephew off the odd thing. He might regret pushing him too far.

"Last time I checked, Liam didn't fuck up in Venice, causing a bloodbath in Naples that meant I had to recruit a whole new crew," he said, quietly and firmly. "Also, I don't remember him moving too quickly over here and nearly getting himself killed. That's not even taking into account Giovanni and Dolly. Your cousin and friend are buried in the woods because you won't listen to my words. Is it any wonder I've stopped wasting them on you?"

Marco gripped the chair arm. "That was not my fault. I'll take the first two. Don't you dare put their deaths on me. They were friends of mine."

Shaking with rage, Marco glared at him. Lorenzo realised he'd gone too far. "All right. All right," he said, placing his hand over his nephew's white knuckles. "I'm sorry. But can you understand? All your life, I have wanted this for you. You're too headstrong, Marco. You need to learn to be calm once in a while. Rage isn't the only way to solve a problem. I want you to learn to think about a situation before you go dashing in there. I can't be any clearer."

Marco's eyes welled up. "I did my best for you, Uncle."

Lorenzo patted his fist and got up. "I know you did. You aren't learning, though. This is a real problem for me. You must see that."

Miserably, Marco nodded.

"Then you come in here and question why I'm doing something?" Lorenzo continued. "Acting like a jealous brat about your own boyfriend and your uncle? This is not good enough, Marco." Marco had the good sense to keep quiet. Perhaps he did listen. "So, from now on, you report to Federico."

Marco reared up as if a shot had gone off. "What did you just say?"

"I think you heard me perfectly well."

"Do you know what this looks like?" Marco's face burnt bright red with rage.

Lorenzo had expected this reaction. Ignoring the slight twinge of guilt, he met Marco's stare. He would test his nephew as he saw fit. Marco had a choice to either handle it or not. "Yes. I don't care and neither should you. Federico is analytical and calm. You will do well to observe and learn." He sympathised with the dejected Marco. He had brought it on himself and not every lesson could be sugar-coated.

"I understand," Marco managed.

He probably wanted to say a million other things. *Credit to him for swallowing down his indignation.* "Well done," Lorenzo soothed. "I believe in you, Marco. I know what you need. You just have to trust me."

Marco nodded.

"Your grandfather trusted me. I came back to Rome with bullet scars in my back and a broken bloody heart, but he knew what I needed — to focus on the business and learn everything he could teach me."

Curiosity replaced Marco's upset. "A broken heart? You never told me you had a lover here."

"Not worth mentioning." Lorenzo sniffed. "Papa wanted me within the bosom of the family after that. He'd always had this in mind for me, like I have for you. One day, you'll rule this mob. I promise you that. It's yours to lose—it always has been. Although please don't tell Fed, Gab and Tom that just yet."

Again, Marco nodded. "I will earn your trust, Uncle Z."

Lorenzo grinned. "You have my trust already, little one. I just need you to earn my confidence."

He had called him *little one* since he had been born. Marco blushed. "Don't call me that in front of the others. Being demoted to Fed's lackey is one thing. I'd never lead after that."

Lorenzo chuckled. "I promise, I won't. Now scram. I've got things to do."

Marco got up and crossed the small room to the door. "Can I ask you something?"

"Of course."

"What happened to your lover? Did they kill him too?"

The concern on Marco's face warmed Lorenzo's heart. "Don't worry about him. Everything will come together in the end. Of that I promise you."

Realisation dawned on Marco's face. "Is there where you went this morning? To meet him?"

He was astute. Lorenzo would give him that. "Some things are my business, little one. When the time is right, I'll tell you everything. Now off you go and make yourself useful somewhere."

Marco nodded and closed the door behind him. Lorenzo took a long drag on his cigarette and exhaled, watching the smoke disappear into the air.

His body still felt alive at seeing Harry. He'd known it would be a strange sensation but hadn't expected this yearning that had set up home in the pit of his stomach ever since he'd seen him. Lorenzo thought he'd packed his feelings for Harry away years ago. Seeing him, smelling him and touching him had unlocked the door instantly.

He wondered if Harry was struggling with the same emotions. Lorenzo found himself desperately hoping that Harry would still be trustworthy, even after all these years. What if there was still something there? Was it too much to hope for?

"Come back to me," he whispered.

Chapter Four

"What do you get if you eat Christmas decorations?" Lorenzo asked.

They all stared at him in silence.

"Tinsilitis."

Silence fell over the room except for a groan from Liam.

"I don't get it," Lorenzo said, holding the piece of paper up.

"It's a joke." Liam giggled. "As in *tonsill*itis."

Frowning, Lorenzo peered inside the broken cracker then emptied a plastic cow and a paper hat into his hand.

"This is a strange bloody country," Federico said. "It must be the lack of sunlight."

"Or the food?" Tommasso chipped in.

"Hey," Liam said. "It's not all bad. There's…well…pie and chips."

Everyone around the table started to protest until Lorenzo held his hand up. "He has no idea, boys."

"You're woefully outnumbered, my love," Marco said, kissing the back of his hand.

"Just put your hat on," Gabriele directed Federico.

Federico unwrapped his own hat and put it on his head. It didn't sit all that well on top of the gelled spikes that he spent each morning perfecting. *"Buon Natale."*

They all burst into laughter.

The house was packed. Lorenzo had realised it was unfair to expect the lads to spend Christmas Day in a campervan so, in a fit of Yuletide madness, he'd ordered them all into the house. They had bedded down in the lounge and once more the bedrooms were full to the brim.

Now they sat around the kitchen table, full of merriment, while others were in the hall at a makeshift table they'd made out of Enzo and Paolo's abandoned gym equipment and an old door. It looked fine with a sheet over it.

The atmosphere was light and fun. Lorenzo valued the sacrifice they were all making for him, being here and not with their families, so he'd lavished them with lovely gifts and food.

He noticed Liam's smile falter. "Missing Shaun?" he asked.

Liam's brother Shaun, along with one of Lorenzo's best men, his nephew Enzo, had set off into the sunset a few days earlier. They'd fallen for each other in a big way. Unlike Liam, Shaun refused to be a part of this life. Lorenzo thanked his lucky stars there weren't any more Moseley siblings to ruin his plans.

Realising they needed help, Lorenzo had given them both a way out—his villa in Tuscany. It worked in everyone's favour. If things went wrong in England, Lorenzo might need an escape route. Either way, Shaun was going to set up a yoga retreat. A bit of legal money coming in never did anyone any harm.

Liam nodded. "I'd set my heart on us spending Christmas together this year."

Marco sat on the other side of Liam to Lorenzo. He filled up his glass. "Maybe we can have Christmas in Tuscany next year? What do you say to that?"

Liam's eyes lit up and Lorenzo could see the child that he once had been. "That would be great," Liam said. "Can we?"

Lorenzo nodded. "Of course. You can visit your brother whenever you like."

Getting up from the table, Liam grabbed his mobile phone. "I'd better go and call him."

Marco watched Liam walk out of the kitchen door. Claire, Liam's best friend, followed him. She had barely spoken since Lorenzo had known her. "Is she all right?" he asked Marco.

Marco shook his head. "I don't think so. I've tried to talk to her, but she just clams up."

Lorenzo nodded and stood. The lads stopped talking and stared at him. "This is a party," he said. "Out in the barn is a case of wine. If you're not on a guarding shift, then what are you waiting for?"

Some of the lads cheered and got up, racing one another out of the door. Lorenzo shook his head and followed them into the yard. Liam stood out in the field on the phone, but Lorenzo could see no sign of Claire. He put on his thick jacket. It had been the first thing he'd bought in town after he'd left Harry.

He cleared the side of the house and saw Claire walking up the top field. She disappeared over the brow of the hill. He knew exactly where she would be going.

Lorenzo set off in pursuit of her. As he left the pandemonium of the house behind him, his thoughts turned once more to Harry. Seeing him again had made Lorenzo feel like the last fifteen years hadn't happened. What was he doing today? He would be with Jonny. *Where else?*

Now they had to wait until his quarry showed himself. Jonny had gone to ground. Marco said that he had gone full paranoid about his daughter getting caught up in things again. She had nearly been burnt alive when Marco and Liam had attacked Jonny's house.

Lorenzo hadn't heard a thing from Wellingham... Did that mean Harry had kept his secret? If he had, surely that had to be the first chink in the armour? He hardly dared hope for that.

Out of breath by the time he reached the top, Lorenzo leant against a tree. He was getting out of condition. Once upon a time, he would have been able to run up this hill with no effort.

Above the brow was a cluster of pine trees. The smell filled the air like an alpine spa. In the centre was a clearing with an outcrop of rock protecting it from the elements. Claire stood by a piece of ground that had been disturbed recently. He came near to her. She whirled around when she heard him coming.

"Relax," he said, holding his hands up. "It's only me. I hope you don't mind me intruding. I can go."

She wiped a tear from her eyes and shook her head. "You probably own this wood anyway, but no, I don't mind."

The sale for the farm wasn't quite complete. Lorenzo didn't think now he should be splitting hairs. "Are you okay?" he asked. "I'm sorry, ignore my clumsy words. Of course, you're not."

"I miss her," she said, simply.

Lorenzo put his arm around Claire's shoulder and pulled her close. He let her cry it out. Very early on, he had learnt to let emotion come. Too many people bottled it up until it overpowered them. Especially in this bloody country. Over the years he had seen many friends die. He had become very familiar with negotiating grief.

"This is an unforgiving life," he said, when she stilled.

"How do you stand it?"

The ten-million-dollar question and one he didn't have a true answer for. "I was brought up for this. There was never any discussion about what I would do. It's the same for Marco, Fed, Gab and Tommasso."

She moved away from him. The guilt at her and her friend having been caught up in his world still smarted Lorenzo. "I want to be useful, Lorenzo. I can't mope around here anymore. If Jonny Wellingham is getting what he deserves, then let me be a part of it. For Dolly if nothing else."

He hugged her. "That's the spirit. In fact, I have a little job for you and you alone. Do you think you could do it?"

Claire frowned. "Depends on what it is. If you're after a Christmas blow job, you can fuck off."

Lorenzo threw his head back and howled with laughter. "My love, I'm sure you're very adept at what you do, but you're not my type. No, I need you to get a message to Shola Rose. I want a meeting with her and this Greg Brooks guy. Liam can find him."

Shola Rose was the biggest madam in the northwest and Greg Brooks her counterpart with drugs supplies. Lorenzo needed to ramp things up and going to the top was the only way to ensure Jonny didn't gain a foothold in his old market.

"What are you up to?"

He looked at her. "We're going to chop Jonny up from every angle. When we're finished, he'll be lucky to get a job sweeping the bloody streets."

His mobile vibrated in his pocket. *There's no fucking peace. Even on Christmas Day.* The display told him the call came from Marco. He'd left him just minutes ago. "I'm only in the wood," he said. "What is it?"

"He's out," Marco said.

"Get everyone ready," Lorenzo replied. "I think it's time to wish an old friend a happy Christmas."

Lorenzo cut the call.

"What is it?" Claire asked.

"The rat has come out of its hole," Lorenzo said. "Come. Let us get our finery on. I want you with me."

* * * *

He was looking pretty sharp, even if he said so himself. Lorenzo had put on one of the new suits he'd had shipped from Milan before they'd arrived. In a midnight blue, it shimmered. Marco looked so handsome in a grey suit and Liam scrubbed up well in a black one that Marco had given him. He'd never worn a suit before and his eyes fairly sparkled when he came down the stairs. Underneath it all, he was just a kid who needed to be loved. Amidst all this chaos, Marco had found a wonderful companion. How did that happen?

Claire got out of the SUV. She shone in a bright red form-hugging dress and blazer.

"You look wonderful," Lorenzo said.

She shrugged. "It was one of Dolly's. I've pinned it up. I wanted a part of her to see this."

He nodded and kissed her on the cheek. "This is for them and us."

Christmas music sang out. The restaurant had spared no expense with the decorations. An elaborate nativity scene dominated the entrance foyer, lit and complete with floating angels. Every table had a centrepiece of baubles and holly while every available space was strung with golden lights that gave off a wonderful glow. It fairly cheered Lorenzo's heart. Or that could just be the exhilaration at finally coming face-to-face with the biggest piece of shit he'd ever met. Customers filled the place. That gave Lorenzo and his boys all the cover they needed. Even a nutter like Jonny Wellingham knew better than to start a shootout in a packed restaurant on Christmas Day.

Tommasso and Gabriel made up the rest of the party. Three lads were in the driving seats of the SUVs they'd arrived in.

"Keep the engine running," Lorenzo said. They might need a quick getaway. He had no idea how Jonny would react to this bombshell.

Marco opened the door and they all followed Lorenzo in. Nobody paid any attention to them. The diners seemed intent on celebrating the festive day. Lorenzo vowed to himself that this would be the last time people didn't stop and say, "There goes Lorenzo de Luca."

A waiter stopped "Can I help you?"

"We're here to see Jonny Wellingham," Lorenzo replied.

The waiter nervously took them all in. "Mr Wellingham isn't…"

A maître d' cut in. "I'll deal with this. Hello, Marco."

Marco stood at the side of Lorenzo. "Hello, Stan. Where are we going?"

Stan glanced around. Satisfied they wouldn't be overheard, he nodded his head. "The door next to the toilets. It's a private dining room. He's got lads."

"As have we," Lorenzo replied.

Stan considered Lorenzo with interest. "And who might you be?"

"Time will tell you that," Lorenzo said.

Marco dug into his pocket and palmed the man a wad of bills. "Get your family something nice in the sales, yeah?"

They marched through the restaurant. People were now realising they weren't just normal customers here to celebrate Christmas and watched them nervously.

That's more like it, Manchester. "Very good, little one," Lorenzo murmured. "You've established connections. I'm impressed."

Turning a corner, he saw the sign for the toilets and a doorway to the left.

"This must be the private dining room. Tommasso and Gab, stay next to me in case that mad bastard tries anything. Marco and Liam, I want you near the door. Don't let them trap us." He held his arm out for Claire. "Young lady. Would you care to join me?"

Linking his arm, she nodded. "For Dolly."

They swept into the room. A large round table sat in the centre and two figures at the door stood in front of them.

"Who the fuck are you?" one demanded.

"Your worst nightmare," Lorenzo replied. "Now get out of my way." He saw Harry at the table and butterflies took flight inside him. As if sensing something, Harry glanced over in their direction. The shock on his face was worthy of a frame.

Next to him, with his back to the door, sat a figure Lorenzo would know at fifty paces. It might have been a decade and a half, yet he would recognise the wiry frame of Jonny Wellingham anywhere.

Anger pulsed through his system as he barged past the lad on the door.

"Hey, you can't just come in here," he shouted after him.

This caused Jonny to spin around, and they locked eyes. To Lorenzo's joy, he saw absolutely no recognition from Jonny as he and Claire sauntered up to the table.

"She doesn't work for me anymore." Jonny sniffed, scowling at Claire. "If you've got a complaint."

Lorenzo stopped and smiled down at Jonny. "No complaint from me. I just came to wish you a Merry Christmas."

Jonny got up and scowled at him. Lorenzo could practically see the cogs whirring in Jonny's mind—he clearly recognised him and couldn't place where from. "Who are you?"

"Oh, that will come to you," Lorenzo said, enjoying himself.

He scanned the table. Harry and a couple of lads he didn't know were looking at him full of concern, and a young woman sat on the other side of Jonny. That had to be his daughter, Sadie. Although scarred from where she'd been burnt in the fire, she was still a beautiful girl.

The scowl she sent his way contradicted that beauty. *Like father, like daughter.*

"Bit careless of you to be here," Claire muttered.

"What did you say, whore?" Jonny barked in retaliation.

Quick as a flash, Lorenzo slapped him hard across the face. Jonny staggered away, his hand coming up to his jaw. Poor Jonny seemed genuinely shocked. The two lads at the table stood. Tommasso and Gabriel were over in no time. They shoved each Wellingham Boy into their seats, holding them firm.

"How fucking dare you?" Jonny shouted. "You have no idea who I am, obviously. I've a good mind to put a fucking bullet in you."

His moment had arrived, and he had every intention of enjoying every last bit of it. He reared himself up to his full height, which admittedly compared to Jonny wasn't much. "You tried that once," he drawled. "As usual, you fucked it up."

Jonny frowned. "Who the fuck are you?"

"Surely you haven't forgotten your old pal, Lorenzo?"

Realisation dawned on Jonny's face, and he took a step away, holding on to his chair for support. "What the…" Jonny's mouth opened and closed.

He glanced to Harry for support, but Harry kept his head down. Lorenzo's soul danced that Harry hadn't given him away. Jonny wouldn't be faking. He wouldn't want to be seen so weakened in front of his crew.

"B-but…" Jonny stammered.

"You okay there, old man?" Lorenzo chuckled.

"How?"

"Your dickhead little mob you sent to kill me didn't check they did the job properly." Lorenzo sneered. "You always were lazy."

Jonny glanced over his shoulder and must have registered Liam and Marco. "This was all you?" he snarled.

"Just a little aperitif, Jonny, my old mate," Lorenzo continued. "Now you've upset my friends and we can't have that."

The colour rushed into Jonny's face now although he had started sweating. "What the fuck you going to do?" he demanded. "This is my city."

Lorenzo shook his head. "My nephew took you down with six people. Imagine what I'm going to do with an army."

Gabriel and Tommasso were by his side now. They were tall and solid, far superior to the youngsters who were cowering around the table. Even Jonny took another step back.

"I killed two of your pathetic little rejects," Jonny spat, clearly trying to regain the upper hand. "I'll do it again."

Claire launched herself at him, gouging lines in his cheek with her nails. Almost immediately, Sadie leapt out of her seat, hauling Claire off Jonny. With a nod from Lorenzo, Gabriel and Tommasso sprang to action, Tommasso dragging Sadie off Claire while Gabriel stood in between them.

Jonny ran his hand over his face and examined the blood. "You stupid bitch. How you're going to regret that."

"The only thing I regret is seeing your weasel face, Jonny Wellingham," Claire shouted. "Your days are finished. You're out-classed and you know it."

"How dare you lay your filthy fingers on my father," Sadie screamed. She struggled to get free from Tommasso, but he held her firm.

"You think it's the first time he's touched a whore?" Claire snapped. "Ask your mother about that."

"Sadie," Jonny bellowed. "Sit down."

She sat in her seat and scowled at Claire.

"That's good," Lorenzo said. "You've learnt some decorum. A shame your daughter hasn't."

"What do you want?" Jonny asked. He grabbed his napkin from the table and mopped his sweaty brow. He threw it back down on the table and glared at Lorenzo. "Well?"

Lorenzo leaned in so close to him that he could smell his rancid aftershave. "Everything."

Chapter Five

There were more than a few thick heads the next day. When they'd got back to the farm, Lorenzo had declared a victory party and they'd drunk everything within reach. The younger lads were having a dance-off when Lorenzo finally called it a night. Lying on his bed with the room slightly spinning, he'd gone to sleep wondering what Harry's reaction to his dramatic reveal would be.

It had just gone nine in the morning and Lorenzo sat at the table in his bathrobe nursing a coffee. His head was splitting and his body felt as though a football team had played on it. Hangover aside, things were on the up. Seeing Jonny's face the day before had made up for fifteen years of waiting. The icing on the cake had been that Harry hadn't warned him. Lorenzo had trusted him, and Harry had come through.

Even in a situation like yesterday, Lorenzo's body had still betrayed him with Harry there. His palms had sweated like a teenager's asking a girl to the dance.

Harry had done that to him when they were together and surprisingly, he still had the ability to throw Lorenzo off kilter.

Ever since he'd returned to Italy, he'd had men. In fact, a steady line of them had made their way to his bedroom. Most didn't last longer than a week. There had been one guy who he hoped he might be able to have a relationship with, but when he'd found out what Lorenzo did for a living, he'd headed straight for the hills.

The door opened and a very rough Marco sloped in. Lorenzo gestured for him to sit down and poured him a coffee. "Jesus." Lorenzo slid the cup across to him. "You look like I feel."

"Ugh," Marco replied. "I feel like death. Vodka is going to do Jonny Wellingham's job for him one of these days."

"We had fun, though, didn't we?" Lorenzo smiled.

Marco nodded then winced. "Yeah. My body is telling me I had a lot of fun."

They sat in companiable silence for a while. Marco had Lorenzo's dark curls and dark eyes. Unfortunately, they also shared a temper, a tendency towards impatience and a big mouth that got them into trouble on a regular basis. Those things were easy to harness and direct. *Passion should never be extinguished.*

Once more his thoughts fell to Harry. He'd meant what he said. Before he finished Jonny for good, when the bastard fell to his knees, begging Lorenzo for mercy, he'd find out who had told him Lorenzo was gay. Wellingham was only half of the deal.

"What are you thinking about?" Marco asked.

Lorenzo snapped out of his daydream and clocked his nephew watching him intently. "Revenge of course. What else?"

Marco sipped his mug, cradling it like he'd used to as a child. "Then what?"

It had been harsh making Marco report to Federico, but Lorenzo wouldn't go back on it until he could be absolutely sure there would be no repeat of the stupid mistakes recently. People had lost lives due to Marco's impatience. The stakes were too high.

"I think I'll go to Tuscany," he said. "You can only live like this for so long. I'm ready to step away from things." The expression on Marco's face made Lorenzo burst out laughing. "Your ambition is showing, young man."

"You know I want it," Marco said. "I would be lying to you if I said I didn't."

Lorenzo nodded. "Then watch and learn from Fed."

They were disturbed by a sleepy Tommasso coming into the room. Lorenzo hoped to God he hadn't been listening at the door. He wouldn't put anything past him. Gabriel was loyal to the end and Federico had the sense to stay on the side of strength. Tommasso could be a loose cannon. He always had been.

"Morning," he said, slumping down next to Marco.

Lorenzo poured him a coffee which he handed over. "And how are you this morning?"

"I've been better," Tommasso said. "And I've been worse."

"Cryptic," Marco muttered.

Lorenzo sniggered which made Tommasso glare at them both.

"Always the funny guy," Tommasso muttered under his breath.

"What was that?" Marco snarled.

"What's happening today?" Lorenzo asked Marco. Hopefully his tone made it clear to both of them to knock it off. He had no desire to get in the way of a slanging match. His poor head couldn't take it.

"The girls are doing a double shift at the Riverside apartments," Marco said. "So many wives fuck off to the sales, leaving their husbands bored and horny. Claire says it's usually a busy one."

"Who's running security?" Lorenzo asked.

"I'm going down in a bit," Tommasso said with a yawn. "I'll take the two of the lads least likely to puke, when they get up."

Lorenzo frowned. "Do you mean the girls are there on their own?"

Tommasso shrugged. "It's not even ten o'clock yet. I bet it's only taxi drivers around anyway. Let me have my coffee first."

Leaning forward, Lorenzo tried his best to hold his temper. "In case you missed it, we served Jonny Wellingham notice yesterday. Do you think he's going to just take it? He's a nasty bastard and he will come out fighting. Fucking hell, you can see that in his daughter. She's as mad as he is."

Tommasso grinned. "She's fit too."

"Jesus Christ!" Lorenzo shouted. "If you could think with your brains instead of your dick, I'd be eternally grateful. Go upstairs and get two of them up. I want you there within the hour. I mean it, Tommasso. This is no time for slacking."

Tommasso drained his cup and put it slowly down on the table. He smiled at Lorenzo. "Your wish is my command, Uncle."

Maintaining his slow moves, designed to inflict maximum annoyance, he left them to it. Lorenzo cursed every footstep he placed on the stairs. "He's pissing me off," he muttered. "Did you know about this?"

Marco held his hands up. "Not guilty. I asked him yesterday and he reckoned he had it covered."

"Then you should bloody check," Lorenzo spat back.

The hurt that washed across Marco's face made him instantly regret it.

"You said I should stick to Fed," Marco mumbled. "I told him. Never let it be said I don't know my place."

He'd turned his own actions on him, the crafty sod. Lorenzo sighed. "The responsibility is mine. I'm sorry for shouting."

The sound of Tommasso raising hell upstairs made his headache cut through him like the carving knife they'd used on the turkey. He didn't fancy a day of telling the lads what to do or where to go.

"Here we go," Marco said. "When one is up, the rest will be."

"Tell you what," Lorenzo said. "How about we commandeer the lounge today? Gab can take the lads who aren't working out on a big walk. Tire them out."

Marco raised an eyebrow. "Won't that come across as favouritism?"

"Probably." Lorenzo grinned.

Federico came downstairs. "Who put a bomb in Tommasso's ass?"

"That would be me, because you left the girls unprotected," Lorenzo replied.

With eyes wide, Federico looked at Marco. "Shit. You did tell me. I'm sorry, boss. Do you want me to go with him?"

Lorenzo shook his head. "It's a bit late now. Tommasso can handle it."

"I really am sorry."

Marco had triumph written all over his face. That rankled Lorenzo yet he could hardly argue. "You can go and get supplies. Are you okay to drive?"

Federico reached into the fridge and got out one of his energy drinks. "Sure. I didn't have much."

Always the sensible one, as a child he'd read his books while the other tore around Papa's estate, hollering and getting into fights. Methodical and logical, he had become a great asset to Lorenzo. They had achieved a lot together.

"Fed," Lorenzo said. "Can you tell Gab we need peace in this house today. He can take a few on a walk."

Fed nodded. "What are we doing?"

"Movie morning on the sofas," Marco replied. "When you get home from doing your chores."

Fed's face lit up. "What movie?"

"Nothing space-related before you get any ideas," Lorenzo said, ignoring Fed's instant disappointment. "It's still Christmas—how about *Die Hard*?"

Marco and Fed cheered.

"Where's Liam?" Fed asked.

"Still in bed, the lazy bugger," Marco replied.

"Leave him be." Lorenzo shook his head. "I bet even Joseph and Mary took it easy today."

"I'll go to the shops now," Federico said. "Diego made a list last night. I can be back before Alan Rickman falls. That's the only bit worth watching anyway."

Lorenzo threw a discarded napkin at him. "That film is a classic from beginning to end."

Fed grinned. "Whatever you say, Uncle."

He grabbed some keys and left them to it. Lorenzo and Marco walked through to the lounge. It was still the Santa's grotto that Shaun and Enzo had made a few weeks ago. Lorenzo wished he'd had more time to get to know Shaun. There would be plenty of time for that when he'd got things properly established here.

Marco fiddled with the huge TV to find the film. Lorenzo's mind strayed to Harry once again. The night before, he had even allowed himself to think about a future for the pair of them in Tuscany. Could he really be that lucky?

Tommasso stuck his head around the door. He still had on that surly grimace that Lorenzo could quite happily wipe off for him. "We're off," he said to no one in particular.

"Good," Lorenzo replied. "Shout Gab down. I've got an idea for him."

Tommasso nodded and left them.

"Fucking idiot," Lorenzo muttered.

They would all be outraged when he finally announced Marco as successor. Marco was the youngest of his nephews. So, it went against every tradition. Lorenzo didn't hold with that line of succession shit. He wanted the right man for the job. In his mind there was no doubt that was Marco. It never had been anyone else.

He and Marco settled on the sofas and began watching Bruce Willis looking ridiculously handsome in a white vest, ready to save the world.

About an hour into the film, a thud from upstairs snapped Lorenzo back to earth. It was followed by footsteps running full pelt down the landing.

"What the fuck?" Lorenzo said.

"It's Liam." Marco leapt to his feet.

"Keep calm," Lorenzo soothed.

They waited until Liam burst through the door. His face told Lorenzo something serious had happened. He held his phone out to Lorenzo. "It's him."

With a remarkably steady hand, Lorenzo took the phone from Liam. He looked down at it. A leering Jonny filling the screen. The vindication in his eyes made Lorenzo's blood run cold.

"What the fuck do you want this early?" Lorenzo said, trying to keep his voice as steady as possible. "We had quite the party last night. Didn't you?"

"I'm not going to lie – seeing you again put me right off my turkey. When I woke up this morning, I said to Harry, I fancied a fuck. Imagine my surprise when I find out there are some whores working at this hour.," Jonny sneered. "No rest for the wicked in Manchester these days."

"Stop pissing around," Lorenzo replied. "If you have something to say, say it."

Jonny must have handed the phone to someone because they panned away. To his horror, one of their girls, Debs, sat on a bed. Next to her stood a middle-aged man in his underwear.

"Looks like she has a punter with her already, lads." Jonny cackled, clearly getting into his stride, his eyes wild. "Mind if we jump the queue? The lads need a bit of fun."

Lorenzo saw the room had about five young men in. He scanned around but saw no sign of Harry. That didn't mean he wasn't there.

The farmhouse lounge filled with the sounds of screams coming from the phone, as the lads moved in. One grabbed Debs by the hair and slapped her violently around the face. Another lad held the punter from behind while Jonny himself punched him straight in the guts. They let the man fall to the floor, coughing for all he was worth.

Lorenzo didn't take his eyes off the screen once. He wouldn't give Jonny the satisfaction.

Where the fuck is Tommasso? He should be there by now!

Jonny grabbed Deb's face. "Not bad-looking. I broke her in, you know," he said to the screen. "Is there nothing you won't steal from me, you Italian piece of shit?"

Jonny punched Debs square in the face as they all watched helplessly. She fell to the floor, joining her punter. They had the good sense to stay there.

Thankfully Jonny hadn't done too much damage. Debs would have a black eye and her punter some sore ribs. Lorenzo silently prayed that would be all they would get away with.

"Okay, lads," Jonny said. "It's Christmas. We'll go easy."

Then his face filled the screen again.

"You're going to regret that," Lorenzo snarled.

"This is only the beginning, de Luca," Jonny replied. "You dare to disturb my Christmas dinner? You can kiss my fucking arse. Although you'd probably like that wouldn't you? Expect more of the same."

The line went dead, and Lorenzo threw the phone onto the sofa. He paced over to the door.

"Gabriel," he shouted.

"He's out with the lads," Marco replied.

"Then get him. I want him down there," Lorenzo replied. "Double security on the flats and here. That bastard isn't getting another opportunity. I could bloody swing for Tommasso."

The rage tasted metallic on Lorenzo's tongue. He would quite happily rip Jonny limb from limb. "Marco," he shouted after his nephew who had only got to the door. "Get Tommasso on the phone as well. I want to know where the fuck he is."

Marco nodded and dashed out of the room. Liam came over and perched on the end of the sofa. "It wasn't too bad," he said, trying to soothe Lorenzo.

"Not too bad?" Lorenzo did not feel like being calmed. "He beat up a girl and her customer. That is pretty bad. If word gets out that we can't protect our operations, we're fucked. This is a small town, Marco."

He lit a cigarette and exhaled loudly. It wasn't unexpected that Jonny would retaliate. He hadn't imagined him to be so forthright about it. He must be really annoyed if he was willing to get his own hands dirty.

"I want every idea you have for what we do in response to this," Lorenzo said. "Whatever it takes, that bastard will pay for his audacity."

Liam nodded. "Let me go and speak to Claire," he said. "She should know."

Lorenzo waved him away. He needed some solitude to get his head around this. Liam gently closed the door behind him.

Throwing his half-smoked cigarette in the fireplace, Lorenzo strode over to the window. It was a wild day outside with the wind whipping through the trees, but it paled in comparison to the fury that raged within him.

He needed to strike Wellingham hard as quickly as possible. His retaliation would show Wellingham he wasn't playing around. So far, he'd only thrown verbal threats at Jonny.

His peace was shattered by his phone vibrating.

What now?

His stomach lurched when he saw Harry's name on the display. "You have a fucking nerve," he said, answering it.

"I need to meet," Harry replied. "Tomorrow."

Chapter Six

The plastic-covered tables had seen better days, as had the grim man behind the counter. The smell of chip fat and bacon frying made Lorenzo worry he would never get it out of his favourite wool coat.

He should have known better than to wear it. He had wanted to give the best impression possible. He'd have to ask Diego to order him a new one if the dry cleaners couldn't work their magic.

"Coffee? White or black?"

As much as he would have liked a shot of espresso, that would not be on the menu here. "Black, please," he replied.

The man regarded him with wary eyes. "Food?"

"Can I wait until my friend arrives?"

"You can do what you like," he said before sloping off.

Lorenzo found a table at the rear of the grimy café. Harry wouldn't be best pleased if he arrived to find him in the window, this being a secret assignation. He might be a stranger in town, but Lorenzo also had no desire to be seen in this dump. The de Luca image would never recover.

He wondered why Harry had asked to see him. Probably to try to warn him off retaliation. If that were the case, he was wasting everyone's time. Deep down, Lorenzo hoped this to be pleasure instead of work. He hadn't been able to get Harry out of his mind. At night, when he lay in bed, he remembered all the times they'd shared. The laughs, the adventures and the sex. Oh yes, the sex.

Then the figure of his memories appeared at the door. Lorenzo sat up straighter, his body giving that familiar jolt when he saw Harry. God, he looked good. Not able to contain his beam, he wasn't surprised when it wasn't returned. Harry would be worrying.

Lorenzo didn't care. He luxuriated in seeing him again—after fifteen years, he could never take it for granted. *Has Harry found himself in exactly the same boat?* It would take wild horses to drag it out of him. Poor Harry always did let his sensible nature get in the way of a bit of fun. *That was why we were so perfect together.*

"Hello again," Lorenzo said.

Harry sat at the table and took off his hat and scarf. Mr Misery Guts came over with Lorenzo's coffee that he slapped down, letting it slop into the saucer. He glowered at Harry expectantly.

"Tea," Harry replied.

"Sugar?"

"Two," Lorenzo said. "And milk."

The man glanced at the two of them before shuffling off.

"You remembered," Harry said.

"I remember everything."

Harry smiled for the first time. It made Lorenzo's heart dance to see it. In their previous meetings since Lorenzo had returned, warmth had been thin on the ground. He hardly dared hope things were changing.

"It's been a while since we did this," Lorenzo said.

"Let's deal with the elephant in the room, shall we?" Harry began. "What the fuck were doing coming to Il Migliore?"

Lorenzo picked up the padded menu, careful not to touch the egg yolk crusted on it. "You're surely not telling a Roman that he can't visit Manchester's finest Italian restaurant?"

Harry grabbed the menu from his hand. "Look at me. What the fuck were you doing?"

The only other customers in the place, an elderly couple demolishing huge breakfasts, stared over at them. Harry put his head down. Something had rattled him. Did he really care all that much?

Lorenzo folded his hands and stared at Harry. "I think I made my intentions perfectly clear, Harry. I came to set my stall out and to wish you all a very Merry Christmas."

Mr Misery Guts came with Harry's tea.

"Two bacon sandwiches. Both on white. One with ketchup," Harry said, placing the menu back where Lorenzo had got it from. "You're not the only one who remembers." He watched the café owner retreat before leaning forward. "Two people have been hurt because of your games."

"Not my doing," Lorenzo replied. "Your glorious leader is the only one who can take credit for that. Or was it your idea?"

Harry took a sip of his tea, his hands shaking.

"This is going to build and build." Harry ignored Lorenzo's question. "You'll do something in retaliation, then he will and so on until we're all bloody dead."

Harry had a confidence about him that he hadn't had when they were younger. It made him all the more attractive. Shaking his head, Lorenzo played with the cup in front of him. "And you came here to talk some sense into me? You always were the peacemaker between us two. Shame you couldn't persuade him not to kill me."

"Of course I came to try to make you see sense."

"Bullshit. You came to see me like I came to see you. Because we can't resist. Let's not kid ourselves."

Once more Harry unsuccessfully fought a smile. "You're probably right. It's not every day someone comes back from the dead."

The idea that Harry could even begin to feel as strongly about him as Lorenzo did about Harry was music to his ears. "You didn't give me away either," he said.

"Don't read too much into that." Harry sniffed.

Lorenzo loved this, Harry trying to deny something they both knew had woken again. "Too late." He grinned. "I've read all I need to."

"You always were a cocky fuck."

"I remember when you loved my cock. Amongst other things."

Harry glanced around. The elderly couple were once more engrossed in their fried delights. Leaning forward, Harry lowered his voice. "You're talking about a million years ago. Before you let me think you were dead for fifteen years."

Guilt snapped at him like a crocodile's jaw. If Harry had any idea how many times he'd been tempted to pick up the phone. "And what would you have done if I put you right? You'd have told Mr fucking Wonderful and I would have been looking over my shoulder for the rest of my life."

Harry began to say something, then stopped.

"I'm right, aren't I?"

"Perhaps." Harry took another sip of tea. "We'll never know. I might have run to you, and we could have spent the rest of our lives together."

Nice fantasy. "Oh, Harry. You were never a runner," Lorenzo said with a chuckle. "Remember the time we got busted dealing in that club by the universities? I practically had to drag you out of there."

Harry joined in his amusement. "We ended up pretending we were with the DJ. Fuck, we didn't give a shit, did we?"

"We ruled the world," Lorenzo replied. He loved sharing these memories with the only other person in the world he could do that with. Of course, he'd told people in Italy bits. That time in his life had been so swathed in darkness that most of the time he acted as if his Manchester years never happened. It hurt less.

"I wish I'd gone with you," Harry said. "I wish you'd given me the chance."

Lorenzo shared that dream. It tugged at his heartstrings for the lost opportunity. Harry couldn't be fully trusted, then and now. When Lorenzo had told his papa what had gone on, it had taken all his persuasion not to send a squad to finish everyone off. *What would be the point?*

He had done it to protect Harry. Then, when he'd felt strong enough to tell his father about his sexuality, the time had passed. They built a business that operated in all of Italy's major cities. Revenge had to be put on ice.

"Come away with me," he said.

A shocked Harry shook his head. "You're a bit overdue with that."

"I don't mean forever. Let's get out into the countryside," Lorenzo said. "Miles away from here where you're not jittery in case you're seen."

"Are you crazy?"

"That's what you used to like about me. Remember?"

Harry chuckled. That old spark in his eyes that used to shine straight into Lorenzo's soul ignited. They had been the perfect foil for each other. Lorenzo would come up with a crazy idea and Harry, after a bit of persuasion, would be a willing accomplice.

"You're not wrong there. Some things never change," Harry said.

They stared at each other for a second.

"Go on," Lorenzo said. "I dare you."

Harry sighed. "Jonny would kill me."

"Then don't fucking tell him," Lorenzo urged. "Don't tell me he's got you chipped now?"

Harry bristled at his comment. "Of course not," he said quietly. "I'm taking a risk being here with you. If he found out..."

Lorenzo ran his foot up Harry's leg, enjoying seeing him jump at their contact. "Risks are fun," he whispered. "Isn't that what we used to say?"

They were interrupted by two plates of bacon sandwiches being plonked down.

"Thank you," Harry said.

Lorenzo nodded. Revenge and now the glimmer of reconciliation had brought him to England once again.

Cuisine had not. The greasy, undercooked meat between two doorstops of bread made him want to heave. Did he really used to eat that shit?

"I was an idiot in those days," Harry said, taking a bite. "I'm older and wiser now."

Lorenzo picked at the crust. "You're saying all the right words. Problem is, I don't believe them."

Harry huffed, his eyebrow raised.

"Come on," Lorenzo chided. "I bet Jonny is still sleeping off his turkey."

Harry sighed. "Fine."

Lorenzo clapped his hands together. "I figured you'd give in. I did expect I would have to pay for lunch first."

"You're still paying for lunch, you arrogant fuck." Harry smirked.

* * * *

"Where are you going?" Marco asked, frowning at the small overnight bag Lorenzo carried to the door.

Lorenzo had hoped to sneak out and do this by message. *Busted.* "Oh, I've got to go somewhere. Bit of business."

Marco scanned the hallway. "Who's going with you?"

Lorenzo did not want to do this right now. "I'm going on my own. Honestly, Marco, I'll be late."

Marco, who blocked the doorway, had a cheeky grin on his face. "I know what this is." He giggled.

Lorenzo sighed. "And what exactly is this, Mr Know-all?"

"It's your lover." Marco leant against the doorframe, folding his arms. "It's written all over your face. That's where you snuck off to yesterday as well? I'm right, aren't I?"

Lorenzo sighed and dropped his bag. "So what if it is?" He folded his arms too. "I'm a grown man, remember."

They both burst into fits of laughter. Marco pulled Lorenzo close for a hug, which a surprised Lorenzo returned.

"I'm pleased for you, Uncle," Marco said, clapping him on his shoulder. "He's a lucky guy."

Lorenzo wriggled out of his grasp and went to grab his bag. He could just imagine the change in mood if he confessed exactly who he intended to meet.

"Not so fast," Marco said. "Tell me. Is it serious?"

"Marco," Lorenzo replied, testily. "We've met twice. It's nothing. I just enjoy spending time with him, okay?"

Marco stared at him in a strange way. "Bullshit," he declared. "You have a glint in your eye. You're falling for him again, aren't you?"

This stopped Lorenzo firmly in his tracks. Just as he'd formed a scathing response, he found he couldn't speak the words. He couldn't be falling for Harry again—he'd seen him twice to speak to. He was in his forties, for goodness' sake. Gone were the days where he fell in love in a heartbeat. Gang bosses didn't do that. He put his excitement down to two old friends reacquainting themselves and ignored the fact that he'd been obsessing over what to wear for hours.

"I'm not falling for anyone or anything," Lorenzo said. "This is a side project. Don't forget the main prize. That is what I want you thinking of instead of what I may or may not be doing at night."

"Whatever you say, Uncle," Marco said, still grinning.

"You're impossible," Lorenzo replied gruffly. He had a smirk on his face even so. "Tell Fed he is in charge, ably assisted by your good self. Try not to break anything while I'm gone."

As Lorenzo made to leave, Marco grabbed his arm. "Be careful, yeah? Text me now and again, just to know you're safe."

Lorenzo nodded. "I love that you care. Thank you, Marco."

"I love you, Uncle. No matter what."

"Then you'll keep my secret. I'm serious. I don't want the boys thinking my focus isn't one hundred per cent on Jonny Wellingham. They've sacrificed a lot to be here with us. We must set an example."

"Your secret is safe with me."

As he left the house, Lorenzo's heart soared. Being with nearly all his nephews was wonderful. Of course, he desperately missed Enzo and Giovanni. When things quietened down, he would arrange for his sister to come and visit the grave. She needed the closure.

His relationship with Marco, however, had always been more like that of father and son. They had a bond that couldn't be broken, something Jonny didn't have with anyone. It made Lorenzo powerful, knowing he had his unconditional support.

No matter what.

Getting into his car, he caught sight of himself in the rear-view mirror. He had an inane grin on his face. "Get a grip of yourself, de Luca," he muttered.

Seeing Harry again making his whole body quiver. Even if they squabbled most of the time. That had been their relationship all those years ago. The first time they had slept together had been after an argument...and the most intense sex of his life.

Lorenzo's cock stirred when he thought of it—Harry riding him until the morning. There had been many since. No one that made his balls ache like they had been doing since he'd first clapped eyes on Harry again.

In an act of supreme arrogance, he'd booked a room at the local pub where they were meeting for a walk.

Your move, Harry.

He fired the car into life and set off, anticipation running through his system.

Chapter Seven

The Yorkshire countryside lay before them. It made him think of the view from the farm multiplied by about a hundred. The stunning landscape stretched for miles. "Wow," Lorenzo panted. He really did have to do something about his fitness levels. "That view makes it worth it."

The uphill climb had been a struggle, to put it mildly.

"I told you," Harry said, his breath annoyingly regular. "You need to quit the cigarettes. You're not getting any younger."

Indignation bristled over his body. "Do you mind? I'm in my prime. I still get compliments."

"I'm sure you do, my friend," Harry replied. "You're still my sexy Italian. Despite the wheezing."

To his horror, Lorenzo felt in danger of blushing. His usual bravado and pomp dissolved with Harry around. Just like it did back in the day. "Coming from you, that's a high compliment," he said.

Their eyes lingered just a shade too long until Harry broke the contact. "Let's walk over to that crag," he said, averting his gaze. "I bet the view is different."

Lorenzo wanted to say that as long as he had Harry in front of him, the view would be fine, but even he knew that was way too corny. Instead, he followed Harry along the narrow footpath that connected the two rocky outcrops.

It gave him the opportunity to really take Harry in. He had on criminally tight walking pants that clung to his butt. Lorenzo licked his lips as he watched Harry's powerful thighs carry him over the uneven ground.

"Stop checking out my arse," Harry said, over his shoulder.

"In those pants? Seriously?"

"They're the only ones I have, honest."

A likely story. "I'm not complaining," Lorenzo replied. "Believe me, there's no issues from behind here."

They got to the spot and wandered out onto a platform of volcanic rubble. The valley spread out below them. Harry's theory was proven right—it was even better than the last one. They could have been walking on air.

The winter wind bit. Lorenzo kept snug in his duck down parka. Liam had been right making him get all the gear for life in the North of England. Wool coats would not cut it in the depths of Yorkshire.

"It really clears the head, doesn't it?" Harry said.

Lorenzo took in a lungful of the air. "Just what I need after a hard week plotting your boss's downfall."

Harry spun around. "For fuck's sake. Can't you go more than an hour without mentioning Jonny?"

Lorenzo held his hands up. Typical of him to ruin the moment with a pathetic comment. He wanted to rip his own tongue out sometimes. "Hey, hey. Calm down. I'm sorry. I didn't mean it. It was a joke."

The wind blew Lorenzo's hair into his eyes as Harry wiped a tear from his eye.

"We were supposed to be having a day for the two of us," he said. "I missed you so fucking much, Lorenzo. I still can't believe you're stood here in front of me. I don't want him to ruin it."

Lorenzo stepped forward and drew him close. He luxuriated in the smell of him as he nestled into his neck. "It is just us," Lorenzo whispered in his ear. "He can't get to us out here. I'm sorry."

It had started to rain a little. Harry made to move but Lorenzo held him close.

"We should get to the cars," Harry said.

"Just a little more," Lorenzo said, closing his eyes. If he never got this chance again, he wanted to savour it, his face centimetres from Harry, Harry's breath warm on Lorenzo's face.

Unable to resist any longer, he leant forward and for the first time in fifteen years, their lips met. His heart danced as Harry pressed his body to him, opening his mouth for Lorenzo's tongue. At that point, the passion he had thought long dead exploded and he kissed Harry frantically.

It seemed the feeling was mutual as Harry ran his hands through Lorenzo's hair while Lorenzo held him as close as possible. All those nights of dreaming about what it would be like to do this had led up to this moment and Lorenzo's heart soared.

Suddenly, Harry leapt away. Lorenzo staggered at the shock of being dragged out of his reverie.

"I can't do this," Harry said, clutching at his head.

Lorenzo walked forward, but Harry held his hands up. "No, don't."

"What's the matter?" Lorenzo asked. Confusion and anxiety racked his entire body.

"I can't do this because.... I gave you away to Jonny."

The words hit him harder than any icy wind. Lorenzo stood, staring at Harry in disbelief. Words he had never expected to hear had just blown in on the Yorkshire gale. "What did you just say?"

Harry sobbed freely now. He didn't make a move to try to comfort Lorenzo from the shock of his confession. Instead, he stood there, helpless in front of him. "It's true. It was my fault and I've never been able to forgive myself."

Lorenzo could hardly focus. "How? Why would you do that?" Rage overtook everything inside him. How could Harry even come here just to drop that on him?

"He'd already started to suspect something about you," Harry began. "He'd just got married. It was his wedding when the penny first dropped. You got shitfaced and were way too flirty with me."

Lorenzo remembered that Harry had ended up putting him to bed. Lorenzo rarely lost control. That night, he'd hit the champagne hard.

"It got to be a fixation with him. He never stopped banging on about it," Harry said. "You remember me telling you."

Harry had used to get so stressed about it. He'd worried for Lorenzo but also for himself. They had argued plenty about it. Harry had been nagging Lorenzo to get a girlfriend to throw Jonny off the scent. Typical Lorenzo refused point blank.

"It happened that night. He kept saying terrible things about you. I just sort of snapped."

Lorenzo could barely believe the words he was hearing. Out of all the people in their world at that time, he'd never suspected Harry to be the one who practically signed his death warrant. "Snapped by telling him about me to try to get the heat off you?"

Shock spread across Harry's face. He stepped forward and took hold of Lorenzo's hands. "No, nothing like that," he implored. "I snapped because I hated listening to all these awful names he called you and I just said so what if you were, you were our friend and deserved better."

Harry held on to his hands tightly now, his eyes boring into Lorenzo's.

"And that was enough for Jonny to finish me?" Lorenzo asked. "Fucking hell."

"They shot you an hour later." Harry sobbed.

Lorenzo found he harboured no blame towards Harry. To think that he'd carried that guilt around for fifteen years broke Lorenzo's heart.

Stepping forward, he took Harry in his arms. Poor Harry actually cried out when Lorenzo did this, sobbing into his chest. Lorenzo held him as tightly as he could. The rain lashed down now, but Lorenzo couldn't have given a shit if a tornado had swept past.

He nuzzled his face against Harry's. "None of that was your fault," he murmured. "You loved me, and you are only human. There's only one person responsible. I daren't say his name seeing as I got roasted mere minutes ago for doing that."

The joke brought some badly needed levity to the situation. Lorenzo's hair stuck to his head while the rain dripped off the end of his nose. "Can we go back to the car now?" he begged. "It's getting worse."

They set off down the path. The car might have been only a fifteen-minute walk but battling the elements made conversation impossible.

Lorenzo used the time to straighten his head out. His instant reaction remained true. He didn't blame Harry for this. Their kiss had reignited something powerful inside him — this had suddenly moved past exploration of an old friendship.

The conflict would only increase tenfold when they returned to Manchester. He should drop Harry at his car and drive away. It would be the thing he would tell any of his lads to do in the same situation.

Then his eye caught Harry's hopeful stare as they reached the gate leading to the car park and he was lost. With the car in sight, they ran the rest of the way and by the time they got in, both their teeth were chattering.

"Fuck," Harry said. "It's freezing. Get that heater on. We can at least attempt to dry off before we have to drive home."

Lorenzo switched on the ignition and glanced at Harry. "In a moment of optimism, I booked a room at the pub in the village we drove through. I thought...well...anyway, we can at least use it to warm up in and dry our clothes."

Harry raised an eyebrow at this. "Still the cockiest bastard around."

* * * *

The fire crackled into life. Heat would soon be filling the room.

"You should have plenty of logs."

"Thank you, Mr Durkin," Lorenzo said, shaking his hand.

"Call me James," the handsome landlord said. "Can I get you anything else?"

Lorenzo glanced over at Harry. "You hungry?"

"Yeah. First, I need to get out of these clothes. I'm frozen."

"How about I get Chef to send up some nice bits for you?" James said. "I'll put a decent bottle of red with it."

"That sounds perfect." Lorenzo smiled. "Better make it two bottles. Put it on the tab."

James nodded and left them, closing the door softly behind him.

"If we drink two bottles of wine, we won't be able to drive," Harry said.

"Shame, that," Lorenzo replied with a grin.

Harry shivered.

"Come on," Lorenzo said. "We need to get out of these things."

"Together?" Harry asked.

Lorenzo ran his finger down Harry's cheek. "I wouldn't leave you out here shivering while I got undressed. It wouldn't be fair."

"Who says...." Harry began before chuckling when he realised the joke. "Very funny."

"Yes, together, you fucking idiot," Lorenzo said. "Unless you have something I haven't seen before?"

Harry shoved him towards the bathroom. Instantly, Lorenzo's bravery deserted him. He worried that Harry thought it was just that. *Undressing.* He desperately wanted more and just knew his body, or rather his cock, would betray him if he clocked Harry stark naked.

They got into the small wet room. With shaking hands, Harry fumbled with the buttons on his shirt. Lorenzo reached forward and helped him. Harry stared into his eyes and moved his hands away, letting Lorenzo have free access.

His heart racing, Lorenzo undid the top button. He never broke their gaze as he flicked open the second, then the third. His cock had totally forsaken him now and strained against the confines of his trousers.

Grazing his knuckles against Harry's breastbone, he could swear he felt his heart beating just as hard.

Reaching his waistband now, Lorenzo took hold of the shirt with both hands and tugged it off Harry's torso. He had bulked out since their twenties, and it suited him. His chest was a mass of solid muscle. Lorenzo longed to reach out and stroke his abs. He still didn't trust that this to be a green light.

Letting Harry's shirt fall to the floor, he dragged his own jumper over his head. He threw it down and was about to do the same with his T-shirt when Harry's hand stayed him. "Can I?" he asked.

Lorenzo nodded.

Harry took hold of his T-shirt and dragged it over his head. He stared at Lorenzo's body, no doubt replaying memories in his head in the same way that Lorenzo was.

Now, he'd got through that. He wanted to be here with Harry now. Not as a trip down memory lane.

Harry reached forward and undid the top button on Lorenzo's trousers. Harry's fingertip tracing along his boxer shorts set Lorenzo on fire. "You might get a surprise down there," Lorenzo said, making no effort to hide his hard-on.

"Show me," Harry urged.

Lorenzo undid his trousers and let them fall to the floor, stepping out of them and his socks at the same time. He stood in front of Harry in just his tight black boxer shorts, his cock protruding because he was an absolute lost cause now.

Harry took his own clothes off, kicking them away. Lorenzo palmed his cock as he watched him reveal more of his body. The fact they'd only had one kiss made this all the hornier. The delicious yet bittersweet taste of anticipation.

It didn't take long until Lorenzo had drunk enough of that. He pulled Harry to him by the waistband of his boxer shorts and kissed him. Cold skin melded together as he wrapped him in his arms. Their cocks rubbed and he took a step back to steady himself on the vanity unit.

Harry wrapped his arms around Lorenzo's waist and let his hand wander across his arse. Lorenzo moaned into the kiss at the touch.

He couldn't wait for this much longer. Pushing Harry against the other wall, he switched the shower on, and warm water cascaded from the monsoon above. It sent shockwaves through his body as he hungrily kissed Harry.

He tugged at Harry's briefs, pulling them to the floor. He never broke their kiss in dragging his own off and pressing his hard cock against Harry's. God, it felt so good to be totally skin on skin.

"Oh fuck," Harry groaned as they broke the kiss.

Lorenzo kissed his neck, nibbling and licking. Harry lifted his foot, hooking it around Lorenzo's arse and grinding against him.

Suddenly a loud knock reverberated throughout the room. "What the fuck?" Lorenzo panted.

"Room service," came a voice.

To his horror, the door in the bedroom opened. He made it across that bathroom in breakneck speed. Unfortunately, not in enough time to save the poor man coming from getting an eyeful.

Lorenzo unsuccessfully attempted to cover his still-hard dick with his hands and smiled apologetically. "Sorry."

Chapter Eight

A burning log crackled in the fire. Lorenzo and Harry lay in the little nest they had created for themselves. Once Harry had managed to control his laughter and the apologetic staff member had retreated, Lorenzo had commandeered the duvet and pillows off the bed.

It was fun having a naked picnic in front of the roaring fire. The landlord had done them proud, sending up meats, cheese, warm bread, olives and the best bowl of chips Lorenzo had had in years. They were so good they'd calmed his carnal thoughts for a minute or two.

Now, as Harry lay in his arms, nursing a second glass of red, they were resurfacing. He traced his finger along Harry's shoulder.

"Did you lock the door?" Harry murmured.

"I certainly bloody did," Lorenzo replied.

Harry chuckled. "That poor man's face."

Lorenzo kissed the top of Harry's head. "It probably gave him a thrill. I bet they don't get much of that round here."

Harry stroked Lorenzo's body. He ran the tip of his finger lightly over the hair on his chest, tracing a line down his happy trail. Once again, Lorenzo's cock sprang to attention.

"What we were talking about," Harry said quietly. "How can you not blame me for telling Jonny? Everything that happened was my fault."

Drawing him close, Lorenzo inhaled. He wanted to remember his scent again. "Because you were only acting like a human being. That man has a way of pushing people to breaking point. I know that as well as you."

Harry moved up so he sat on his haunches, his eyes wet with tears. "What are we going to do?"

Leaning forward, Lorenzo kissed him. "I have quite a few ideas, if you'd care to try them out. I'm sure we aren't that out of practice."

"I didn't mean..."

"Harry, we've waited fifteen years," Lorenzo said.

There would be plenty of time for soul searching later. What Lorenzo needed right now didn't require words. He moved so the duvet slipped from his body. His cock had risen to the challenge again and this time he didn't want any interruptions. He gave his whole body up to Harry to do with as he pleased.

Harry reached down and tenderly took Lorenzo's cock in his hand. Lorenzo gasped at Harry's touch and how he used his other hand to stroke his inner thigh — a sensitive area on Lorenzo. It made his heart sing that Harry had remembered that. "I need you," Lorenzo whispered. "Come here."

They kissed, Harry crouching over Lorenzo, one hand still massaging his cock. Lorenzo brought his hand up and rested it on his shoulder then stroked his biceps. Harry's skin was soft to the touch.

As he straddled him, Harry's hole brushed against Lorenzo's cock.

Please don't come now, de Luca. You want so much more.

Harry's hard cock rubbed against Lorenzo's belly, and Lorenzo ran his hands down Harry's body, resting on his hips. The next kiss they shared was more passionate. Lorenzo probed Harry's mouth with his tongue.

The sensation of kissing Harry had such a powerful effect on him. His whole body responded, sending tingles around his system. He'd never expected this would happen again. Lorenzo had resigned himself to a life of meaningless sex and making money. With Harry in his arms once more, everything had changed.

He sighed as Harry placed light kisses on his neck. Harry travelled down to his nipple, worrying it between his teeth. Lorenzo had always been sensitive there too, and he gasped, gripping hold of Harry's head.

Harry flicked his tongue lightly over him before moving farther down. Once more, Lorenzo's body bristled with anticipation as he writhed underneath Harry. How he needed this.

Harry continued his journey along Lorenzo's stomach. Lorenzo's breathing became shallow as Harry reacquainted himself with every inch of his body.

Lorenzo jumped as Harry placed a light nip on his hipbone. "Oh yes," he whispered.

His cock ached for attention. Harry nestled his nose in the downy hair, smelling his scent. Lorenzo watched him, the care he took sending him into orbit. He hadn't been this turned on in years.

He nearly came right then as Harry blew lightly on his cock, the head dark red as it flushed with blood. Ever so gently, Harry ran the tip of his tongue along the ridges.

Lorenzo couldn't take much more of this.

Harry had other ideas and traced the vein down to the base, making Lorenzo cry out again. Harry continued to his balls, running his tongue around one then the other. Lorenzo spread his legs wider, giving Harry all the access he needed.

The wait was killing him, but just to have Harry's hands on his body meant he wanted it to last forever.

Sitting back on his heels, Harry looked at him. "Fuck, you're perfect," he whispered.

They stared at each other's bodies. Harry's dark, muscular body and Lorenzo's light, wiry one. They had both kept themselves in shape and fitted together like a jigsaw.

Reaching forward, Harry grasped Lorenzo's cock again at the base and with a final glance into his eyes, he guided it into his mouth. The heat enveloping his cock made Lorenzo cry out and twist the duvet in his hands. Sensation ran throughout him as Harry sucked.

When Harry paused, the slow and steady approach went out of the window. He fell onto Lorenzo, their mouths crashing together. Lorenzo grabbed the back of his head and held him there as he pushed his tongue into Harry's mouth.

They rolled over on the duvet so Lorenzo lay between Harry's legs. He ground his cock against Harry's as they kissed, the full-body contact making his heart race and his balls ache.

He had hardly dared dream of this moment on the drive over. He'd worried about what it would be like. Would he match up to the Lorenzo in his twenties? *A new sensation for Lorenzo de Luca.* Fifteen years was a long time. Would they still fit together so well in bed, like they had all those years ago?

He needn't have worried. If the last few minutes were anything to go by, they seemed to be even better.

He took his turn to explore Harry and didn't want to miss a thing. Moving so he crouched on his knees, he ran his hands across Harry's skin. It gave him a kick seeing gooseflesh appear at his touch. Harry's skin had remained so soft. Lorenzo wanted to touch every part of him, to reclaim him for his own once again.

Can that ever really happen?

Harry's hard cock leaked pre-cum. Lorenzo rubbed his thumb over the tip, causing Harry to murmur. He brought it up to his lips, tasting him. "You are incredible," he whispered.

Then he bent down, taking Harry's cock in his mouth. The salty taste exploded on his tongue as he ran it around the head.

Harry moaned as Lorenzo sucked him. Lorenzo travelled down his thick shaft maddeningly slowly. If Harry wanted to play that game, then so be it.

Reaching the base, he held it there for a second before he sucked him hard, running his lips up and down Harry's solid dick. Harry grasped his curls, pumping his hips. Lorenzo had never had sex this intense. Not even the first time they had found themselves in bed together all those years ago.

He let Harry's cock fall out of his mouth and lifted Harry's legs, exposing his hole. God, he remembered how much he had loved that part of him.

Tracing his tongue along Harry's balls and down the seam, he licked hard. When he reached his ass, Harry cried out. Lying flat, Lorenzo lapped at him, his tongue making Harry's body judder with each pass.

Harry held his own legs and spread them. Lorenzo ran his finger over the now wet hole. He pressed gently, letting the tip breach Harry.

"Fuck," Harry whispered.

Lorenzo wouldn't be able to fuck him. It would be over in seconds. Besides, he wanted to focus entirely on Harry's pleasure.

Reaching up, he took hold of Harry's cock and stroked it as he licked his arse. The noises coming from Harry suggested he was doing everything perfectly.

Then Lorenzo moved his head so he took Harry's cock in his mouth once more. With his free hand, he pressed more deeply into his hole.

"I won't last," Harry managed.

This only made Lorenzo suck harder at Harry's cock. He didn't want Harry to last. He wanted every last drop of him. Lorenzo's head bobbed up and down frantically as Harry thrashed against the duvet. He let his legs go so his feet rested on Lorenzo's shoulder blades.

"Oh, God. Lorenzo…"

Harry's orgasm exploded in his mouth, the thick salty cum sending his tastebuds into overdrive as he swallowed it all down.

When Harry's body had stilled slightly, Lorenzo let the spent cock fall from his mouth and crawled up his body. He kissed Harry's panting mouth, enjoying letting him taste his own cum on Lorenzo's tongue.

Straddling Harry, he took Harry's hand and brought it down to his own cock that desperately needed some release. Harry had regained enough composure to start to tug. With his other hand, he kneaded Lorenzo's arse cheek.

Lorenzo bucked his hips in time to Harry's moves, fucking his fist. He threw his head back, stretching his body and loving that Harry would be taking it all in. "Oh fuck," he murmured.

His orgasm built as Harry expertly guided him. Gripping Harry's ankles, he bent his whole body backwards. Then it hit like a freight train. Lorenzo came hard, his cum shooting from his hard cock and falling on Harry's sweating skin. His body overcome with the emotion, he tensed every muscle, riding the sensation. He cried out, feeling the exquisite pleasure in every pore.

When he returned to earth, Lorenzo fell forward and kissed Harry.

He had waited so long for this, and he had never sex like it. All the others paled into insignificance compared to the touch of this man. They always had. He realised that now.

* * * *

Lorenzo marvelled at the feeling of Harry in his arms. He kissed the top of Harry's head as they lay listening to the sounds of a rural village. Sheep calling to one another, birds singing and an argument in the next bedroom. "There's no bloody peace in the countryside, is there?" Lorenzo grumbled.

Harry cuddled into him. "After that, I'm not sure I'd ever sleep anyway. God, it's good to be in your arms again. How has this even happened?"

Lorenzo was content for the first time in years, the waves of pleasure gently cascading over him. The people he had slept with in Italy had mostly done so because of his reputation. They expected him to be strong and brave. Harry had seen deep into his soul, and he wasn't afraid to show him again. Except...

"It's going to make it harder. You do realise that?" Lorenzo said. "Being on opposite sides, I mean."

Harry's body tensed. "Don't ruin it," he mumbled.

"I'm not," Lorenzo said. "It's a fact. We can't hide from it."

Harry lay quiet for a second before raising his head and gazing into Lorenzo's eyes. "Jonny's got a project on at the moment so he'll be distracted. I'll be able to sneak around a bit."

Lorenzo didn't like the sound of this. "What bloody project?"

"Don't ask me things like that," Harry said. "I'm not being go-between. Do whatever you want to Jonny — I'm past caring — but I won't be used by you, Lorenzo."

Lorenzo kissed him. "Fine. Fine. You can't blame a boy for trying."

Harry nuzzled into his neck. "If you're a honeytrap, then I think I'm well and truly caught."

Spinning him over, Lorenzo lay on top of him. "Good," he whispered and nibbled Harry's neck. "Because this time I'm not letting you go. I don't want to know what he's doing. I do want to know you're safe."

Harry sighed. "You're our biggest threat, so that's a bit rich."

They kissed again then Lorenzo moved back. He wanted to remember every part of this moment. He kissed the tip of Harry's nose. "If you joined us, then I wouldn't have to worry whether this new project put you in danger," he ventured.

Harry shook his head. "You get into my pants and now you're telling me how to live my life? Firstly, let's just chill out and see what happens and secondly, it's a construction project, all above-board, so my life's not going to end this week. Unless they drop a brick on my head."

Lorenzo kissed Harry's chest, running his hands across his hard pecs. "See what happens?" he said. "That sounds positive."

"Shut up and suck my dick," Harry replied.

Now that he could do. As he continued to explore the body that had been denied him for a decade and a half, his mind wandered to what Jonny had up his sleeve. He would get Fed onto that straight away.

Well, tomorrow.

Today he had other things in mind.

Chapter Nine

"He's late," Marco announced for the fiftieth time.

"I wonder if he'll show," Gabriel said. "Wouldn't surprise me if he bottles it."

"He will," Liam replied. "Jonny won't be able to resist. This is his chance to show off in front of his minions."

"I made him think I wanted a deal." Lorenzo grinned. "Jonny Wellingham is fuelled by greed. He'll be all over it. Trust me. He's never been the brightest spark. That's why he needs Harry."

"That bastard," Marco muttered, making Lorenzo bristle.

The Manchester weather had been true to form all day and a thick drizzle soaked the windscreen. Lorenzo wished Jonny had picked one of the many bars in the city centre for their meeting, but he could understand why he had chosen this out-of-the-way location – Jonny wouldn't want any potential punters witnessing a showdown. *Too much violence can be bad for business.*

That meant Jonny was probably rattled by Lorenzo. *So he should be.*

Also, the prospect of seeing Harry again preyed on Lorenzo's mind. He tried to push that distraction away. They'd spent all night in each other's arms in that glorious pub and when the dawn had broken and it had been time to part, it had been agony. Harry wanted to get back to Manchester before anyone missed him. Even with Lorenzo trying his best, he wouldn't be tempted to stay under the duvet.

Two days had passed without Lorenzo hearing from him. He'd spent the time getting the boys to find out what exactly Jonny had going on in the centre of town. When he'd requested the meet, a message had come in from Harry, demanding to know what Lorenzo had up his sleeve.

Lorenzo had ignored him. Harry had been the one who'd made it clear they had boundaries—Lorenzo had no intention of breaking them. Harry couldn't have it both ways. Well, he could have had if Lorenzo hadn't foolishly forgotten to take condoms on their secret night away.

His cock stirred at the notion of unfinished business between them. He wouldn't let that derail him. Today he needed his brain, not his groin. "Is Fed in position?"

"Yep," Marco said. "If he tries anything, we're covered."

They had spent the previous evening going over the plan to the point where everyone was sick of talking about it. Even so, nerves jangled around Lorenzo's system. He didn't know how Jonny would react once things got in motion. If he realised Lorenzo had the upper hand, it could make him unpredictable. After

Naples, Lorenzo liked to know they had everything covered.

He'd suspected Jonny would be late, a vain attempt at grabbing the control of the situation. It would take more than a fucked alarm clock for that. Jonny thought he was fighting the Lorenzo he knew. Fifteen years leading the biggest organised crime operation in Rome had taught him a few new moves.

"He's here," Gabriel said.

"The stupid bastard's fallen for it," Lorenzo said. "Tell Tommasso to give it five minutes then move in."

They got out of the SUVs and walked up the little path to the edge of the canal. Houses and workshops lined the towpath. Jonny had chosen the place — no one would disturb their little meeting. With a canal in between them, the chances of things descending into violence were limited.

"Jonny's learnt something," Lorenzo said. "When I worked for him, he'd have ambushed us somewhere. Then we would have had to kill him. Damn."

"This will be Harry's idea," Liam said.

Lorenzo's ears pricked up at the mention of Harry's name. "You think?"

"Definitely," Liam replied. "It's him all over."

Lorenzo hated the idea that Harry and Jonny were plotting against him. Even if it were just for show, Harry would have been trying to second guess him. How long they could go on living this double life concerned Lorenzo. Something would have to give at some point.

A fleet of BMWs drew up in the car park opposite. Lorenzo stood with Marco on one side of him and Liam on the other. Gabriel stayed behind them, with ten other lads fanned out along the canal. As a purposeful show of strength, it worked. Even better, he had ten others waiting at home. It didn't do to show the whole hand in one go.

Jonny had clearly had the same idea. Lads got out of the cars. As Jonny got out of the middle car, Harry followed suit. Lorenzo couldn't look at him. His body betrayed him whenever he had Harry close. He yearned to dive across the canal just to touch him.

A scowling handsome heavyset man got out too. He stood next to Jonny as if they were glued together.

"Who's that?" Lorenzo asked. The man had an air about him that Lorenzo didn't like. He was almost chomping at the bit.

"That's Deano," Liam whispered.

Lorenzo had heard all about Deano, Jonny's bloodthirsty protégé. Liam had warned all of them to watch him. If anyone would go rogue, it would be Deano. Lorenzo had met that type before. They got far too much enjoyment out of this life. No doubt Jonny used that to his advantage wherever possible. *Perfect for someone who feared prison so much he'd be in a different town when he sent his lads on missions. Gutless bastard.*

Lorenzo had first met Jonny when he'd been out of prison for a year or so. Jonny had vowed then that he would never be sent back inside again. In fact, the threat of being banged up in a cell was the only thing that truly terrified him.

The rest of the lads spilled out of the cars. Lorenzo could barely disguise the grin on his face. True to form, Jonny had an army that had practically been ripped from their mother's breasts. *Perfect.*

"Good job it's school holidays," Lorenzo said. "Otherwise, it would be Jonny, Harry and his pet dog."

Laughter rippled through their crowd.

Jonny led his little band up to their side of the towpath. He stopped directly opposite Lorenzo. Hatred exuded from every pore. Lorenzo could more than match him in pent-up rage.

"Good morning," Lorenzo said. "I see you're doubling up as a kindergarten these days, Jon. Very community-spirited."

They were close enough to be able to hear a pin drop but far enough away that if anyone made a move, they would be long gone before they made it to the other bank. If this had been Harry's idea, it reinforced Lorenzo's wish that Harry join them. With their two minds working together, nobody would get in their way.

Harry stood next to his boss and Lorenzo didn't dare meet his gaze. The memories of the touch of his skin, the taste of his mouth and the feel of his body were still very much alive in Lorenzo's mind, although not enough to distract from this delicious moment. Having Jonny on the rails was almost as exciting as having his cock in Harry's mouth.

"What can I do for you?" Jonny asked. "Had enough already?"

"Jonny, Jonny, Jonny," Lorenzo said. "I've given you the wrong impression. I've come to make you an offer."

Jonny glanced at Harry who remained stoic. "A deal? From you?" Jonny said the words as though they would infect his mouth. "You must be fucking joking. As far as I'm concerned, you stay around here much longer, and I'll make sure you end up face down again. This time permanently."

Lorenzo cackled. He had got into his stride now. "You failed at that the first go, old man," he sneered. "What makes you think you would succeed with a second try? The times have changed. Surely even someone as thick as you can see that."

Jonny began to reply when movement to his right caused everyone to gasp. Deano rummaged in the inside pocket of his jacket. "Let's just fucking finish him," he snarled.

"No," Jonny shouted.

It came too late. Deano had a handgun out and pointed towards Lorenzo. Before he could even get the safety off, a shot rang out. Blood spurted from Deano's kneecap as he fell to the ground, howling in pain.

Federico was the best sniper in Italy and had positioned himself in the window of one of the abandoned mills lining the canal. Jonny had underestimated Lorenzo if he hadn't warned his pitiful little army that they would be covered from all angles.

"Jesus Christ," Harry cried out. "Is he all right?"

Deano was wailing at the top of voice. Blood had already started soaking through his jeans. The smug grin had disappeared somewhat.

Lorenzo allowed himself a victory chuckle. "No walking for you for a bit," he jeered. "Silly boy."

Jonny hadn't flinched once. "Get him in the car and to the hospital," he said calmly.

He went over to where Deano had dropped the gun and kicked it into the water. It landed with a *plop* and floated down to its final resting place.

Jonny stared at Lorenzo. "He's a bit headstrong," he said with a bitter smile. "No hard feelings, eh?"

"And the same for you," Lorenzo said, returning the fake smile. "Some lessons can be hard ones. You taught me that."

Jonny strode to his previous position so he faced Lorenzo once more. It was the first time he had been able to really examine him. On Christmas Day he had been so taken up with the dramatic return he hadn't had a chance to study his old friend's face. It wasn't a pretty sight.

He had aged badly. His favourite combination of stress, whisky and cigarettes had clearly taken its toll. The skin around his jawline had sagged, giving him a basset-hound appearance, exacerbated by the tan that Liam told him he insisted on keeping up all year round. His thinning hair was greased back in an attempt to recreate his younger style. Yet the mean rat-like eyes were still there. They were exactly the same as when Lorenzo worked for him. Cruelty leached out of every pore in Jonny Wellingham.

Deano made quite a fuss as they got him into one of their cars. Lorenzo had heard that Deano was Jonny's third in command after Harry. He wished he would give him more of a challenge.

"I'll ask you again," Jonny said, "before he brings the law down on us. What do you want?"

Lorenzo glanced at Gabriel, who gave him the slightest nod. It would be imperceptible to anyone who wasn't looking closely enough, but it was more than enough for Lorenzo. "I just wanted you and your little tribe out of the way for a bit," he replied. "And you obliged, you stupid bastard."

Jonny frowned. "What do you mean?"

"Oh, Jonny, you forget how well I know you," Lorenzo continued. "You just had to come mob-handed. Show the world how big your dick is. But you've left yourself weak elsewhere, Jon."

With Deano shut in the car, the silence descended like an audience hushing. They were ready for the main event. He'd known this would be fun but not this much. "A new brothel, is it?" he asked. "The venue to end all venues? I don't fucking think so."

Jonny had started twitching now. Lorenzo loved to see it. He'd also gone a worrying shade of crimson. How poetic would it be if he just dropped dead of a heart attack? *His own rage being the death of him.*

"Check it," Jonny roared to a young man to his side.

Before the poor lad could even make the call, Jonny's phone rang. Lorenzo couldn't have timed it better himself. He didn't even try to control the glee on his face.

"Sadie?" Jonny barked into the phone. "Are you all right?"

The panic in his voice caused Lorenzo to make a mental note. He'd never actually hurt a woman—that had never been the de Luca style. If she was Jonny's Kryptonite, she might be useful. Jonny listened to the voice on the other end of the phone. His scowl rested on Lorenzo, who simply waved sweetly back at him. "Just make sure you're safe," he said eventually. "I'm coming." He terminated the call. "You ever go near my daughter again—"

"Oh, fucking relax. I'm not interested in your nasty little offspring," Lorenzo said. "You're getting careless, Jon. You spilt blood when you came for my nephew. Consider me letting her walk an act of friendship. As for your new venue, I'm sorry it's going the same way as your pool house. Fire can be a very dangerous thing."

"You piece of shit," Jonny said, already edging to the path towards the car park. "You think this is over? You better watch your fucking back."

"Bye, Jon," Lorenzo shouted, waving at him.

Don't Look Back in Anger

He allowed himself to glance at Harry. The scowl of loathing that met him took his breath away. Lorenzo had slightly betrayed his trust, but Harry wasn't in any danger. Surely he wouldn't be making a fuss about this.

Lorenzo just winked at him. He wasn't going to let anyone ruin this moment of victory. He'd deal with that later. Lorenzo had always been able to talk Harry round when they'd quarrelled. Usually with sexual favours…a method he was not averse to using again.

The boys around him all collapsed into fits of laughter as they watched the great Wellingham's Boys dash to their cars and drive into town at top speed.

"Poor Jon." Lorenzo wiped his eyes. "He never was all that bright."

They made their way to the SUVs. Federico waited, the rifle slung over his shoulder.

"Beautiful shot," Lorenzo said, hugging him.

"Thank you, Uncle," he replied.

Liam went up to him and flung his arms around him. "I've wanted to do that for years," he said. "Thank you."

Federico ruffled his hair. "You're in the family now, Liam. It was my pleasure."

"Hands off my man," Marco teased.

"You can't blame the lad," Fed replied as Liam extracted himself from the hug. "He's going for the family member with the biggest gun."

Marco groaned and shook his head. "Big gun, bad jokes."

They all jostled and joked as they walked to their cars.

"What now?" Gabriel asked, when they got there.

Lorenzo had planned for this. He wanted to push Jonny even further. Jonny could be unpredictable—his hit on Dolly and Giovanni proved that. It was heartening to see that his urgency still made him careless. The more Lorenzo provoked him, the more mistakes he would make.

"Liam," Lorenzo said. "Where is Jonny's favourite bar in Manchester?"

"He loves The Roof. It's on the top of an office block and everyone goes there."

Lorenzo nodded. "Then we go there too. We'll drink champagne until we're sick of it."

The lads cheered.

"Are you sure?" Liam said. "It's rubbing his nose in it."

Marco put his arm around him. "That's the point."

They got into the SUV, Gabriel driving with Federico up front, Lorenzo, Marco and Liam in the back. Liam still seemed worried.

"What is the matter, Liam?" Lorenzo asked.

"Jonny will strike hard, you know," Liam replied.

Lorenzo chuckled. "Oh, I do hope so. I haven't even started yet, and it would be a shame if he just rolled over and died. No, I want Jonny Wellingham to fight. It's far more fun that way."

Chapter Ten

The bar at the Hotel Deco had opulence written all over it. After being cooped up in the farmhouse for days on end, Lorenzo relished being free to rediscover Manchester a little bit. After their fun at Jonny's expense, things had gone quiet. Something that preyed on his mind.

Except for setting up this meeting, Lorenzo had had too much time on his hands. Three messages to Harry went unanswered. Lorenzo might have been able to dish that kind of behaviour out, but he'd never been able to take it. Worries plagued his mind at night. Had he royally fucked things up by having to rub Jonny's nose in it?

The hotel was perfect for his needs. It had only sixty bedrooms and lay at the top of a beautiful building in the centre of the city. The bottom floors held a busy restaurant and a concierge sat on street level, with lifts taking customers to the public areas on the upper floors.

Lorenzo had positioned two lads with the concierge. He had been a little put out at first. When the general manager told him Mr de Luca had hired the whole bar and a suite, he soon changed his mind. It never failed to amuse Lorenzo how money could open every door in the world. The trick lay in finding out how much he needed to spend.

Outside on the roof terrace, the rain mercifully held off. Having an open-air bar in this city took a colossal level of optimism.

Liam and Marco glanced nervously at him. In minutes, the biggest drugs distributor in the north-west of England, Greg Brooks and the country's most successful madam, Shola Rose, were coming. Everything had to be perfect. They hadn't got where they were by being easily swayed.

"Are we all set?" Lorenzo asked. He sounded more nervous than he'd intended.

Marco pointed to an office block across the way. Once again, Federico had taken up a position to cover them. Gabriel stood at the reception, waiting for the lifts to come. If it went wrong, it wouldn't be for the want of planning.

Lorenzo took a sip of his champagne and sighed. Once more, Harry popped into his mind. They could be such a powerhouse if they were to join forces. Everyone knew Wellingham would be over without Harry. The bond between Harry and Liam reminded him of the one he shared with Marco. The four of them could do wonderful things. Lorenzo might even defer Tuscany if that were to happen.

Lorenzo couldn't obsess about that right now. He had bigger fish to fry. At that point a hard-looking man and an even harder-looking woman walked out onto the terrace.

Lorenzo stood up and offered his hand to them. "Lorenzo de Luca."

The round bald man with a face that could curdle milk took his hand. Lorenzo had dealt with some hard nuts in his time and sensed instantly it would not do to mess with Gary.

He then turned to Shola. "Can I get you a drink?" he asked.

"Gin," she snapped.

"Gin and tonic?" Lorenzo asked.

"I said gin," she replied.

"Of course you did. Gary?"

"I'll have a pint with you," Gary replied. He had a broad Mancunian accent. Tattoos covered nearly every part of skin on show and a thick gold chain hung around his neck.

"Very good." Lorenzo nodded to Liam to make the arrangements. "Please sit."

His heart pumping as they sat, he enjoyed the rush. There was no way this could go wrong. Lining up his next blow on Jonny made his body tingle.

"I've heard a lot about you, Mr de Luca," Gary began.

"The same for both of you," Lorenzo began. "Liam has brought me fully up to speed. You are the people to know for getting product and girls around here. I'm not sure if you've heard, but Jonny Wellingham is over. I thought it wise for us to discuss the future."

Liam returned with the drinks and sat down next to Lorenzo. He nodded at Gary and Shola.

"I heard you'd got shot," Shola said, sipping her gin.

"I did," Liam said.

"He's fully recovered now," Marco added.

"And you're gunning for Jonny?" Greg asked. "Why?"

Lorenzo appreciated this brand of honesty. He had decided he would match it. He didn't want to pull a fast one on Jonny – he wanted to bury him. "I'll level with you both," he began. "I used to run with Jonny many years ago. He had three bullets put in my back. I've come back to finish him. He's had it too easy for way too long.."

Greg glanced at Shola. Liam had told Lorenzo that they had been business partners for ten years. Rumour had it it went deeper than that. No one had dared to ask. "Sounds a bit personal to me. We don't want to get caught up in a war," Greg replied. "It's not good for business. It attracts attention."

"I understand that," Lorenzo said with a smile. "It's not your fight and I don't blame you for being wary. You've done business with Jonny for years and very successfully by all accounts."

Shola laughed. "We did. Since you came on the scene, that's been disrupted. Why shouldn't we just finish you? There's a lot to be said for it being the better the devil you know."

Lorenzo nodded to Marco, who produced a black leather holdall out from under the couch they were sat on. He slid it over to Greg. "What's this?" he asked.

"Three hundred grand," Lorenzo answered. "I want to buy Jonny's debt to you and give you a down payment on our first shipment. One of many, I hope. You can have the rest once we've shifted it."

Greg nodded. He lit up a cigarette and offered Lorenzo one. Lorenzo took it. He'd promised Harry he would think about giving up. Now Harry had opted for radio silence, Lorenzo would do as he liked. Not that there was anything between them. It had just been a stupid conversation.

He lit the cigarette and exhaled. Greg watching his every move meant Lorenzo wouldn't show any apprehension. He'd dealt with people like Greg before.

"Why would you want to buy Jonny's debt?" Greg asked. "Seeing as you hate his guts?"

"I don't like to think of you out of pocket because of my activities," Lorenzo said. "I would want assurances that his credit is bad. Permanently."

"You're a shrewd bastard," Shola cut in.

"I like to think so," Lorenzo replied. "The bottom line is that the days of Jonny Wellingham are over. The dealers on the street are with us now. They have been for months. I'm sure you can imagine, it's a pain in the arse bringing stock over from Italy. If we do business, it's a win for both of us. You must be missing the Manchester market."

Shola tipped the last of the gin into her mouth. "You're too late, Mr de Luca. Jonny came to see us last week and we did a deal. Sorry."

She got up. Lorenzo noticed Greg faltering. He just needed to get Shola on side.

"Mr Brooks?"

"Shola's right," he said. "Jonny told us he can get the dealers on board again. You selling gear at cost has to stop or we're going to fall out. No one is making profit then."

Marco had been selling at cost for the last few weeks to keep everything ticking along. No matter the uncertainty, the dealers wouldn't say no to taking all the profits. Lorenzo had plenty of cash and it had been worth it to block Jonny from regaining a foothold in the market. A plan that wouldn't make him popular with anyone but the street dealers. However, at the end of the day, they were the critical link in getting product to customers.

"I don't wish to fall out," Lorenzo said. "We've had enough bloodshed."

"We heard about Deano," Shola replied.

Lorenzo took a sip of his drink, studying her over the rim of his glass. That had perhaps been a step too far. Still, Deano had been the one acting like he was in a Guy Ritchie movie. *Stupid lad.* Lorenzo had to remember that in a backwater like Manchester, everyone knew everyone else. It would be just his luck for Shola to be Deano's bloody aunt.

"He had it coming," Liam said. "After what he did."

Shola's beady eyes were fixed on him. "Meaning?"

"Deano attacked our farm," Marco explained. "He killed my cousin Giovanni and Dolly."

Shola sank into her chair. "Dolly's dead?"

"At point-blank range, I'm afraid," Lorenzo said. "That's why I came over so quickly. That bastard needs neutering."

Shola looked absolutely lost for words. Lorenzo would be willing to bet that didn't happen very often. Hope glimmered in the distance.

"She gave me my first start," Shola said, her bottom lip trembling. She held on to the chair arm, her eyes filling with tears.

"Liam, get Ms Rose another gin," Lorenzo said.

Liam dashed off to the bar.

"Why?" Greg asked. "Why did Dolly cop it?"

Marco sat forward. "They attacked our house. Earlier in the week, they had already shot Giovanni in the leg so he couldn't get out. Dolly wouldn't leave him."

Lorenzo read the pain on Marco's face as one-hundred-per cent genuine. The guilt he shouldered for that would stay with him for the rest of his life. If he had sense, he'd channel it. If he didn't, it would consume him. Lorenzo had plenty of those emotions that kept him awake at night.

"Sounds like Dolly," Shola said. "She never said no when you needed help. I...I can't believe it."

Lorenzo didn't want to overplay his hand. If they suspected him of using Dolly's death for gain, they would turn on him like a dog that had been starved. "I'm sorry to have to give you that news," he said. "My nephew tells me she was a very remarkable woman. I'm sorry Wellingham didn't give me the chance to meet her."

Shola glared at Gary. "He can't get away with this. How fucking dare he?"

Gary nodded and stubbed his cigarette out. "All right, Mr de Luca. You've got yourself a deal. Wellingham is finished. I think we can all agree that. I've a better idea than bleeding him dry."

Lorenzo raised an eyebrow. "Oh, yes?"

"Just kill them. The lot of them," Gary replied.

Harry's face instantly flashed before Lorenzo's eyes. As Wellingham's right-hand man, he would be one of the first targets. No matter what the future held, he couldn't let that happen. "No," Lorenzo said, a little too hurriedly. He could feel eyes on him. "There's no need for that. Like I said, there's been way too much bloodshed already. We don't need to be doing long stretches inside because of Wellingham. That really is bad for business. Now I do have a question for you."

Liam put a gin down next to Shola, who knocked it back in one. "Thanks, kid," she said. "What question?"

The pain at losing Dolly had instantly been replaced with a steely determination. The strength this woman exuded took Lorenzo by surprise. She could be a powerhouse as an ally. Plus, it seemed wherever she went, Brooks followed.

"Jonny has new lads," Marco said. "We want to know where from."

Greg smirked. "That's easy. Patrick Bowie."

Lorenzo glanced at Liam who seemed lost in thought.

"From Leeds?" Liam asked Greg.

"That's the one."

"Fuck," Liam said. "He's been mates with Jonny for years. There's no way we'll turn him. He's a nasty bastard too."

Lorenzo took a sip of his champagne. He absolutely would not fall at the last hurdle. "Very well. I have a plan," he said. Shola and Greg stared at him intently. "We'll carry on bringing the stock over from Italy as well as shifting yours. That's double what you're making right now. I'll cut you in if you deal with the distribution from the south. I don't have the men or the time to keep fucking about with that."

Greg nodded. "I like that idea. How does it help you with Bowie?"

"The market might be strong in Manchester, but it can't handle all product we'll be bringing in. I'll promise him the rest at a very good price. It's worth it."

Shola and Greg exchanged a quick glance that told Lorenzo they were thinking about it for a second.

"I'm beginning to like you," Shola said. "Jonny will regret trying to fuck you over. I can see that. What do you need from me?"

This conversation was going better than Lorenzo had hoped. When he scratched the surface, it seemed most people despised Jonny. His papa had always taught him to be decent with the people he worked with because the next day they could be the only thing keeping him alive.

"There are a lot of working girls in town with no jobs," Lorenzo said. "Jonny was going to open some big place in Longsight. Sadly, it caught fire."

"And you were miles away, I'm sure," Shola said.

Lorenzo put his hand on his chest in mock hurt. "I was talking to Jonny at the canal. Couldn't get a better alibi. Anyway, they need work, and we can give it to them."

Shola narrowed her eyes at him. "I've heard about your model. Rent a place for the weekend, make the maximum money then get out of there. I like it."

"Why, thank you," Lorenzo said.

"I'll put the feelers out," Shola said. "We'll sweep them up."

An idea occurred to Lorenzo. "Are any of the girls trafficked?"

Shola gave him one of her hard stares. "I don't get involved in that shit."

"Calm down." Lorenzo held his hands up. "I didn't mean you. I wouldn't put anything past that bastard. Find out, and if they are, we get them home. I won't have that on my books."

It had been a gamble. Shola could be up to her eyes in human trafficking. Lorenzo doubted it. She seemed to have an old-school respect for her profession. As did he.

"You have my word on that," Shola said.

Lorenzo raised his glass. "Here's to doing business together. When can we get the first consignment?"

Gary rubbed his eyes. "I don't want any unnecessary trouble," he said. "Jonny won't just take this, you know. He'll go absolutely crazy if he finds out about this meeting. If things get too hot, I'll kill them all myself. Do you understand me? A war can bring the coppers out."

"You leave Jonny to me," Lorenzo said. "Just get me the stock."

"Okay, Mr de Luca, I'll trust you," Gary replied. "You'll have it by the weekend. Piss me around, and you'll regret it."

Lorenzo allowed a smile to creep over his face. His plan for Jonny had begun to take shape. The smile dropped when he thought about the other man who had come back into his life. Could he even dream of having a plan with him?

Chapter Eleven

The farm had started to get Lorenzo down. Liam's brother Shaun had tried to get it into a liveable condition. Since he'd gone, no one had offered to pick up the project. So, Lorenzo hadn't been able to resist staying the night at the Hotel Deco.

Luxuriating in his surroundings, Lorenzo made a mental note to find the best interior designer in Manchester once Wellingham was out of action. Whether the farm would be his or Marco's, it needed to be far more habitable. He didn't want people thinking the de Luca family were running out of money.

Nothing could be further from the truth. Business was booming back in Rome.

Marco and Liam had gone to the farm with Federico. No one had raised an eyebrow when Lorenzo had told them he intended to stay over at the hotel. He had been fairly vocal about his hatred of communal living. His apartments in Rome gave him all the space he could possibly want.

Of course, Marco panicked about his safety. In the end they had come to a compromise—Gabriel had taken the room across the hall. The chances of trouble were slim. Lorenzo really didn't think that Greg and Shola would play him and Jonny off against each other. There would be no benefit to them doing that and Shola had been genuinely upset that Jonny had ordered Dolly's death.

He didn't like the sound of this Patrick Bowie. From what Liam had told him once they'd been alone, he and Jonny were good mates. Jonny was even godfather to one of Patrick's grandchildren. Lorenzo couldn't understand how anyone would trust Jonny Wellingham with the spiritual growth of their child.

A soft knock on the door disturbed him and Lorenzo's stomach did a flip.

He raced across the room in two strides and flung the door open.

There stood Harry, as gorgeous as ever. He had on a bottle-green coat with a navy sweater underneath, and Lorenzo wanted to rip the lot off him. Ever since they had shared the night in Napthwaite, he had been hornier than a teenager with their first porn mag.

"Inside," Lorenzo whispered, dragging him into the room.

"Nice to see you too," Harry replied. "Fancy room."

"Better than a bloody B&B in the middle of nowhere." Lorenzo shut the door.

They launched themselves at each other. Lorenzo wrapped his arms around Harry's shoulders and drew him in for a kiss. Their lips touching sent Lorenzo's body into overdrive.

Harry pushed him away slightly. "We need to talk."

Lorenzo threw his hands up. "It's always bloody talking with you. I can tell you one thing — that isn't what I need right now."

Harry shook his head. "You can't just pick me up and drop me when you like. You could have got me into real trouble with Jonny."

Lorenzo walked over to the mini bar. If Harry had wound himself up on the way over, Lorenzo needed fortification. "Drink?"

"Yeah, I bloody need one. I was panicking I was going to get jumped at any minute walking in here. Jonny has eyes and ears everywhere. You know that."

Lorenzo poured them both a glass of wine. He gestured to Harry to sit in the sumptuous armchair while he perched on the end of the bed. "Don't be ridiculous. Anyone could have told me about his pathetic building site. He's not the only one with his ear to the ground."

Harry took a swig of his wine. "You know what I mean. I don't want to be guarded when I'm around you, Lorenzo. This has to be different."

He had a point. It had been a low blow of Lorenzo's to use the information that Harry had mistakenly let slip. "Okay. I'm sorry," Lorenzo said. "I shouldn't have done it. Perhaps I got a little carried away. Can you blame me?"

Harry didn't look convinced. He drained his wine glass and continued to stare at Lorenzo.

"Am I forgiven?" Lorenzo ventured, adopting his best little-boy-lost look.

"I'm here, aren't I?" Harry replied. "We must have a rule. No talking about anything to do with you and Jonny."

Lorenzo held his hands up in mock surrender. "Deal. I'd rather talk about you anyway."

Harry got up and stood in between Lorenzo's legs. He pulled him in, so Lorenzo's face nestled against his stomach. The smell of him filled Lorenzo's nostrils and he luxuriated in the feel of Harry stroking his hair.

"I don't know what's going to become of us," Harry said. "Once again, you've turned my bloody world on its head."

Lorenzo stared up at him. "Come to me. I'll protect you."

Harry shook his head and leant down to kiss Lorenzo's forehead. "That isn't not talking about things." He smiled, straightening up. "You lasted about five minutes."

Reaching forward, Lorenzo ran his finger along Harry's waistband. "Seems to me there's only one way to keep me quiet." He opened Harry's belt and deftly undid the buttons on his jeans. Harry was hard and ready for him.

"Oh, yes?" Harry said. "And how's that?"

In one move, Lorenzo dragged Harry's trousers and boxers down. His magnificent dick burst into life, and Lorenzo licked his lips. "My mama told me I must never speak with my mouth full. I might be bad, but I always have impeccable manners."

He wrapped his lips around Harry's hard cock and slid it into his mouth. Harry groaned and staggered a little. Lorenzo held him firm by the waist.

Sucking hard, Lorenzo yearned to take this further. The hotel provided free condoms, so nothing stood in their way this time. Lorenzo quite liked the fact they had unfinished business. Tonight, he needed all of Harry.

Before he took things too far, Lorenzo crawled backwards onto the bed. He yanked his T-shirt off and threw his jeans and socks onto the floor.

"Horny?" Harry asked.

"Like you wouldn't believe." Lorenzo replied, palming his rigid cock.

Harry stepped out of his trousers and took his socks off. Quickly undoing his shirt, he let it fall to the floor and stood at the foot of the bed, totally naked. Lorenzo could only stare, drinking him in.

Tugging his boxers off, Lorenzo threw them across the room. "Come to me," he instructed.

Harry crawled up the bed. Lorenzo sighed as their skin made contact, Harry's cock nestling against his. Their lips met and the kiss was intense. They always were. Today had a deeper underlying passion. It seemed they both knew where it would end up. Lorenzo hoped Harry was yearning half as much as him…then it would be fireworks.

Lorenzo wrapped his arms around Harry's muscular frame, his fingertips exploring every ridge and knot. He ran his hands down so they rested at the top of his arse. Harry ground his cock against Lorenzo's, sending a wave of pleasure through his system.

God, he needed him. Harry sat up, straddling Lorenzo's waist. His cock pressed against Harry's hole.

Drinking every inch of him, Lorenzo ran his fingers all over Harry. His toned skin was silky-soft to the touch.

"Tell me what you want," Harry whispered.

"I want to be inside you," Lorenzo replied. Desire cascaded through him.

Harry slowly rubbed the tip of Lorenzo's cock against his hole once more. Teasing him as to what lay inside. "Inside me? Say please."

Lorenzo pouted. "Please?"

Laughing, Harry kissed him. "The mighty Lorenzo de Luca wants something, does he? I suppose you've waited a long time. I should probably oblige."

Drawing him in for a deeper kiss, Lorenzo slapped Harry's arse cheek. He grinned at Harry. "Ride me."

"Your wish is my command. Did you remember..."

"On the side," Lorenzo said, gesturing to the bedside cabinet where he had placed everything earlier. "I can't wait much longer."

Usually he loved to take time, worshipping his partner's arse and getting him ready. Today, however, the urgency overwhelmed him.

To his joy, Harry reached across and grabbed the condom and lube sachets. Squirming backward, he took Lorenzo's cock in his hand, causing him to gasp. With his other hand, he ripped the condom wrapper with his teeth, pulled the condom out and rolled it onto his throbbing cock. "So amazing," Harry said, seemingly to himself.

Deftly, he applied lube to Lorenzo and before getting into position. Staring up, Lorenzo could have cried at how close he felt to him at that moment. They were bridging a gap of a decade and a half. The last time they had been in this position, they had been young kids, madly in love. Now they were... Well, that didn't matter right now.

Harry let his weight drop, taking the head of Lorenzo's cock inside him.

"Oh shit, that feels good already," Lorenzo moaned, resting his hands on Harry's thighs.

Tentatively, Harry lowered himself all the way down until his solid arse cheeks rested on Lorenzo's thighs. He sat there for a second, his eyes closed, appearing lost in the sensation.

Then he opened them, catching Lorenzo staring. They shared a moment before Harry bucked his hips. Once more, an army of tingles marched over Lorenzo's body, causing him to judder.

Reaching forward, Harry took hold of his hands and entwined their fingers. They were as one now, both fixated on their own and each other's pleasure. Nothing outside of the four walls of the suite mattered.

Matching the tempo, Lorenzo ground his hips against Harry, his tight hole enveloping Lorenzo, the warmth making his balls contract.

"God, you feel good," Lorenzo murmured.

Staring deep into Harry's eyes, Lorenzo realised he would never be able to walk away from him again. Whatever the future held, Harry would be a part of it. Otherwise, what was the point?

Lorenzo rose and supported Harry's back. They kissed fiercely and Harry rode Lorenzo's cock hard. He returned the favour, their hips matching each other in pace and urgency.

"I won't last long," Lorenzo panted.

"I don't care," Harry replied, pushing him back onto the bed

If anything, it made Harry more determined. Supporting himself on his thick thighs, he bounced up and down on Lorenzo's dick, taking him to the edge before plunging down again. Lorenzo gripped Harry's hard cock, letting his own motion create both their orgasms. He tugged harder when his own started to claim him.

"Oh, shit. Harry," he managed.

"Don't let go," Harry urged.

Lorenzo had no intention of letting go. The orgasm exploded out of him, every grind of Harry's hips causing the wave of pleasure to overwhelm him. He was seeing stars and wanted Harry to feel it too.

Always obliging, Harry cracked his head back and painted Lorenzo's body with his own cum. His arse contracted against Lorenzo's spent cock, making him cry out again. Harry's body came to a juddering halt, and he sat still, struggling to get his breath.

That had been intense.

Once they had cleaned up, they lay in each other's arms, basking in the afterglow. Lorenzo could have been floating on air. He had never really touched drugs apart from a little smoke. He had seen first-hand what a mug's game it could be. He wondered if this feeling compared to the highs he had been pedalling all these years. Surely nothing man-made came close to this.

"We've still got it," Harry murmured, nuzzling into his chest.

Lorenzo stroked his head. "We certainly do," he agreed.

"Do you remember that hotel room in Amsterdam?" Harry asked.

In the early days, they had gone on Jonny's behalf to meet a potential weed dealer. He had put them up in the finest hotel with a two-bedroomed suite that dwarfed the one they were in at that moment. Harry had insisted on rolling around in both beds to cover their tracks. He never stopped being a strategist.

"We turned that place upside down," Lorenzo replied.

They hadn't contained themselves to the bedrooms. They had fucked in the shower, on the dining table, the sofas and even the little butler's kitchen. "I don't think any part of that suite got away with us not fucking in it," Lorenzo remarked. That had been quite a trip and all paid for by Jonny Wellingham.

"When you first...well, when I thought you were gone," Harry said. "I used to google that suite. I'd sit for ages thinking about that weekend."

Once more the guilt that plagued Lorenzo reared its ugly head. He didn't regret hiding his existence from Jonny, but he did feel bad that Harry had been caught up in it. "I am sorry," he said. It didn't seem enough but what else could he say? Wishing didn't change the past. It was the future that mattered now. The more time they spent together, the more Lorenzo would fight to make Harry a part of that future.

Suddenly the atmosphere had changed. Harry wriggled up and stared into Lorenzo's eyes. "Turn over," he murmured.

Lorenzo obeyed and rolled onto his front. He guessed what Harry was doing. Gently, he felt Harry tracing around the scars on his back. "I hate that I had something to do with this," Harry said. "If I'd just kept my mouth shut, I could have warned you. We could have run."

Lorenzo moved his head so he could see his lover. "I told you. There is no guilt on your part. Only on his."

"I won't help you. I will say this. Nobody wants you to finish Jonny Wellingham more than me. I will never be free until then."

Lorenzo didn't know what to say. Harry held the key to everything. With his assistance, Jonny would be a sitting duck.

"Why?" he whined, scrambling up to face Harry. "You could put an end to this once and for all."

Harry sighed. "I'm no fool. I know he'd sacrifice me tomorrow. Even so, I have honour. Years ago, I pledged my loyalty to Jonny. That means something to me. I'm not doing it for him. Besides, do you really think he would go down and not take me with him? No, there has to be another way."

The earnest expression on his face mixed with defiance made Lorenzo's heart melt. He ran his hand up Harry's thigh. "I understand," he said. "Truly I do. I don't like it, but I understand it. You have always been too good for this game."

Harry laughed. "I think there might be a few people dead and alive who would disagree with that statement."

Lorenzo had no intention of discussing the sins of the past. "We're none of us perfect. That is for sure."

"Can we…?" Harry began.

Lorenzo took hold of his hand and squeezed it. "Can we carry on meeting?"

Harry nodded, unable to meet Lorenzo's gaze. Lorenzo stroked his cheek.

"Try stopping me," he replied with a grin.

Chapter Twelve

"I didn't expect to be back in Yorkshire so soon," Lorenzo declared.

Liam frowned at him. "When were you in Yorkshire?"

Lorenzo realised his error and shifted in his seat. The SUV zoomed down the motorway and he tapped on the steering wheel nervously. "I...well...I came out here for a drive," he managed.

Liam snorted. "For someone who runs a criminal gang, you're a shit liar."

They burst into laughter.

"It's your lover, isn't it? That's why you went off the other night?" Liam ventured.

Once again, Lorenzo warmed to Liam. It wasn't just that he treated his favourite nephew like a king – his decency and genuine care ran deep. Lorenzo didn't trust many people. He instinctively did with Liam. It didn't matter to him too much that Marco had blabbed to him. Although he would be reminding him that secrets meant just that. "Fine. Have it your way," he relented. "Yes, I met my lover, and no, I'm not going to share what went on."

"I didn't ask you to," Liam said, hurriedly.

"I can reveal a good time was had by all," Lorenzo replied.

"I said I didn't ask you to."

Lorenzo chuckled. Why did the young think they invented sex? He must seem like a dinosaur to Liam. The idea that he was actually sleeping with someone making him turn his nose up.

They were meeting Patrick Bowie at a reservoir on the outskirts of Huddersfield. Shola had arranged the rendezvous but wanted nothing more to do with it. By all accounts there was no love lost there.

The sat nav told him to come off the motorway and they soon found themselves on a small country road.

"We need to have our wits about us," Liam said. "He and Jonny are close. It's not just going to be a case of offering him some cash and he'll do what we want."

"Everyone has a price, Liam," Lorenzo replied. "When that consignment comes in tonight, we'll be set up for months. Loyalty can become an expensive commodity if things are played right."

They were at the reservoir. Two white Lexuses sat at the far edge of the car park. It was a weekday, so they had the place to themselves.

Gabriel and Federico had begged him to let them come. Lorenzo had refused. He wanted to demonstrate trust. He could see no benefit for Patrick in killing them.

He parked up next to the cars. "Keep alert," he said to Liam. "Stay in the car unless I call you. Get in my side. Just in case we need to get the fuck out of here."

He climbed out of the SUV. A squat man in his sixties got out of one of the white cars. About six solid men in their forties and fifties followed suit. Perhaps Lorenzo had been a little too hasty in coming alone.

"Patrick Bowie?" he asked.

"That's me," the man said.

"Shall we walk and talk?" Lorenzo said.

Patrick nodded. He gestured to his men to stay where they were. "I see you brought Jonny's old lacky with you."

"He's a decent lad," Lorenzo countered. "Not a fool who puts all his stake on a lame horse."

They walked up to the wall and stared out over the man-made lake. The wind made the water choppy, and the bite in the air made Lorenzo shiver.

"I presume you've come here to ask me to withdraw my support for Jonny," Patrick asked.

"Partially," Lorenzo said. "Also, to talk business. We have more product coming in than we know what to do with. I'd like you to help us with that."

Patrick stared out over the water. "You know Jonny and I are friends. We go way back."

"I have a history with Jonny too. I'm surprised I never knew you."

Patrick appraised him. "I was in Spain when Jonny took over. I had a little legal trouble. Jon fixed it for me and set me up here. I owe him a lot."

Lorenzo didn't like the way the conversation had headed. Patrick hadn't even raised an eyebrow when he'd offered him a slice of the pie. Unease crept through his system.

"Am I to understand you're not interested then?" Lorenzo asked.

"I won't go against him," Patrick said. "You might be counting him out now. Thing is, I know Jonny Wellingham better than you."

"Then why are you wasting my time?" Lorenzo replied, annoyed.

"Where is the product coming from?" Patrick asked, changing the subject.

Alarm bells rang loud and clear now. Lorenzo set off to walk towards the cars. Patrick stayed next to him.

"You've just told me you're not interested," Lorenzo said. "I'm not likely to give you any information, am I?"

He was still too far from the car to make a run for it. There were three men in between him and Liam. He hoped Liam had locked the doors after him.

"Shame," Patrick said. "It would have made things a lot easier."

"Meaning?"

"For us to find it," Patrick sneered.

It all happened in a split second. Patrick produced a knife out of his jacket and lunged at Lorenzo, but Lorenzo dodged too quickly for him. After diving out of the way, he grabbed the smaller man's hand. It didn't take much effort to hold him in place.

The bodyguards ran towards them. By the time they had got near, Lorenzo had the knife to Patrick's throat. To his relief, he heard Liam fire up the SUV. He just needed to get there.

"Patrick," he said. "That was a stupid move. Don't you know if you pull a weapon out, you have to defend it? It doesn't take much for that weapon to be turned on you."

"You won't get away with this, you Italian fuck," Patrick gasped. Lorenzo had his arm tight around his neck. The difference in height meant Patrick's feet were practically off the floor.

"Put him the fuck down," one of the goons shouted.

"I presume you don't pay them for their brains, then," Lorenzo said.

He practically carried him to the SUV. Patrick struggled until Lorenzo let the knife break the skin on his neck. He cried out in pain.

Once they got to the SUV, Liam opened the passenger door.

"You tell Jonny Wellingham from me, that was a pathetic attempt," Lorenzo snarled in Patrick's ear.

"He doesn't know anything about it," Patrick replied. He tried to struggle but he was like a twig to Lorenzo.

His story made sense. Patrick wanted to show his loyalty to Jonny to get his share of whatever Lorenzo left. He would be Jonny's hero if he'd killed his enemy. He'd come up with a fair plan that he'd executed terribly.

"You've done me a favour," Lorenzo said. "I didn't realise you were quite so amateur. If the lads you've sent to Jonny are anything like that mob of halfwits, I don't need you to remove them. I'll do that myself."

He shoved Patrick forward with his foot, so he fell face forward. Lorenzo leapt into the SUV. "Drive," he ordered.

Liam put the car in gear and floored it out of the car park. Gravel flew everywhere, covering Patrick. Lorenzo saw him being helped to his feet as they got out onto the road.

"What a fucking fool," Lorenzo said. "He'll rue the day he tried that. When we've dealt with Jonny, I want him putting out of business. Do you hear me? No one tries to pull a fast one on me."

They had made it to the main road now. Liam handled the car like a pro while Lorenzo kept checking behind them to see if they were being followed.

However, it appeared that Patrick had had enough for one day.

Once they were on the moors, Lorenzo wound the window down and threw the knife as far as he could. "You did well," Lorenzo said, clapping Liam on the shoulder.

"So did you," he replied. "You were fast."

Lorenzo smiled and looked out of the window at the passing countryside. "There's life in the old dog yet."

Once on the motorway, Lorenzo allowed himself to relax. The threat of being ambushed gone, he could process how he'd been so stupid as to put them both in a position of danger. His mind wasn't fully on the job and it needed to be.

"When we get to the farm, do you want me to set up the office so we can monitor comms on the product?" Liam asked.

"Sure, then I think I might go into town," Lorenzo replied.

He felt Liam glance at him for a second. Thankfully he knew better than to ask him. They drove on in silence. Lorenzo couldn't stop thinking that Harry had known about the ambush.

Then Patrick had said that Jonny wasn't a part of it. The burning question in Lorenzo's mind was if he had, would Harry have warned him?

Juggling the two had become impossible. Things were starting to get on top of him. In the past he'd been solely focused on business. That had worked perfectly. It isn't always easy to close a door you've dragged open.

He needed to speak to someone. Chancing a glance at Liam, he exuded reliability. "Liam, I need to tell you something and I'm so sorry, but you can't tell Marco," Lorenzo said.

Liam's body stiffened. "I don't keep secrets from him. You know that."

"I know, but I need you to this once. It won't be for long. I must talk to you about something that has to remain one-hundred-per cent secret."

They were coming off the motorway to the road that led to the farm. Ever since Shaun had brought gunmen to the little village, Lorenzo and his boys had avoided flaunting their activities or doing anything that might make a law-abiding local get in touch with the local constabulary. At this point, Lorenzo had no desire for any other problems.

"Pull over a second," Lorenzo said.

Liam found a layby. "If you're planning on pushing Marco out," he said, worried, "I won't keep it from him."

Lorenzo's heart melted at the fierceness Liam protected Marco with. When the time came to hand things over to his nephew, it made such a difference to know this lad, wise beyond his years, would be by his side.

He squeezed Liam's leg. "Relax. I would never do that to you. No, this secret is about me, not Marco. Let's say he wouldn't be too pleased."

Liam shifted so he faced Lorenzo. "Now I'm intrigued."

"My lover," Lorenzo began, "is Harry."

If it hadn't been such a serious conversation, the expression of shock on Liam's face would have been comical.

"Fuck," Liam managed.

"Fuck indeed."

"That's why you didn't want Greg to just take out Jonny's mob," Liam said.

It had been that moment when Lorenzo realised he couldn't keep his two lives separate indefinitely. In the past, he would have agreed in a heartbeat and Wellingham's Boys would be past tense. "In business, they would call it a conflict of interest," he said.

"Do you love him?" Liam asked.

"Yes," Lorenzo replied. "I loved him fifteen years ago and I love him still."

Lorenzo didn't know if Harry felt the same or if he saw this as an itch he had to scratch. Lorenzo had come easily to the conclusion that he had once more fallen in love with Harry. As hard, if not harder, than ever before.

Liam ran his hand through his hair. "Shit. That makes things a fuckload more complicated. Why are you telling me?"

This had been a plan that Lorenzo had been mulling over when he should have been thinking of the likelihood of them being attacked at the reservoir. "I want you to talk to Harry. Persuade him to leave Jonny and come to us."

Liam exhaled loudly. "Are you fucking crazy? He nearly killed me, and your nephew is still missing a tooth, in case you hadn't noticed. That might not have been by Harry's hand, but he was still overseeing it."

"Pah." Lorenzo waved the comment away. "That was just business. You were on the opposite side in those days too, if I remember."

Liam seemed stressed at this revelation and Lorenzo didn't like dragging him into it all, but he needed his help. "Harry still thinks highly of you. I know he would listen if you spoke to him."

"Z, if Harry won't do it for you, it's unlikely he will for me," Liam replied. "But we were close once."

"Then it's worth a try," Lorenzo asked. "This isn't an order and if you still refuse, then I will understand. I would consider it a personal favour if you were to give it some attention."

Liam stared into the distance. "Jonny won't allow it. He'd kill Harry before he let him join you. I was nothing to him and he still tried to finish me. Harry knows everything. They've been together for years."

It might be true. Lorenzo had Jonny on the ropes. He wouldn't be a problem for much longer. "Jonny has enough on his plate. And he'll have even more when he can't sell a paracetamol to the clubbers."

Liam scrubbed his face with his hand. "Fine. I'll do it. I don't think I will succeed."

"All I want for you to do is try."

He didn't like putting the lad in this position. But the net was tightening, and he couldn't contain this himself. "Mind you, we're sneaking around in hotels. It's only a matter of time before someone sees us."

Liam frowned. "Why don't you use the flat?"

"The flat?"

"Yeah, Marco is still paying rent on that place in the city centre he had when he first came here," Liam explained. "We…well, sometimes we go there."

Poor Liam blushed.

"I get it," Lorenzo said with a grin. "There's not much privacy at that bloody farm."

They were disturbed by Lorenzo's phone ringing. "It's Marco," he said, punching a button so the speakers in the SUV crackled into life.

"Where are you?" Marco asked.

"Nearly home. Why?"

"Is Liam still with you?"

"Yes, what's the matter?"

"I can't tell you over the phone. You'd better get here."

Lorenzo nodded to Liam, and they sped off up the road towards the farm. "What the fuck now?" Lorenzo asked. "There's no bloody peace."

"It has to be consignment," Liam said.

The thought had already occurred to Lorenzo and a dull ache of worry formed in his belly.

Once they were in the farmyard, Marco waited for them.

"What's happened?" Lorenzo strode across to them.

"The fucking delivery got ambushed at the services," Marco said, under his breath. "They were filling up and it was taken at gunpoint."

Lorenzo glanced from one to the other. *How can this have happened?* "Inside. Now."

They all filed into the office. Some of the lads were playing cards at the table in the kitchen. Once they were in the small room, Lorenzo shut the door. "How the fuck has he found out?"

His mind went into overdrive. He could feel Liam's eyes boring into him. He shook his head. He wanted him to know this information had not come from Harry. He had been far too careful.

"I can't understand it," Marco said. "Only us three, Gab, Fed and Tommasso knew the route. None of the lads have a clue."

Lorenzo sank down in the chair by the desk. The truth stared him in the face. He felt ill at having to confront it.

"There's only one explanation," he said.

"Which is?" Marco replied.

"We have a mole."

Chapter Thirteen

Rage swept through Lorenzo like a tornado. He had been played not once but twice. Someone, a family member, was selling them out to Jonny Wellingham. To make matters worse, Harry hadn't even hinted at this. What had he been thinking? Unless... The alternative was that Harry had played him all along. That was too repellent to even consider at that moment.

Marco and Liam both stared at him, for very different reasons. Marco would be worried about which of his cousins had committed the ultimate sin. Liam would have a far deeper understanding of the situation.

All Lorenzo could think was he needed to speak to Harry. He couldn't believe that Harry would allow him to be in such danger and not warn him. Not after everything they had shared together.

"Okay," Lorenzo said, running his hand through his hair. "Let me think. Not a word leaves this room. It has to be one of three. It can't be you two. If it is, then shoot me now."

There was no way he didn't trust Liam and Marco. Although to think one of his other nephews had sold them out cut him straight into his heart. His papa would be spinning in his grave.

"Why don't we just come out with it?" Marco said. He was bright red and trembling with rage. "We'll be able to tell by their face."

Lorenzo shook his head. "We haven't had a clue so far. They're good. There's no way this can have been going on for too long. We've had Wellingham on the ropes."

Only one course of action lay open to Lorenzo. Unease curled its sharp talons around him. "Marco. We need to move the existing stock. If Jonny knows about the delivery, he'll know where that is. Quickly and quietly."

Marco nodded and slipped out of the room. This left Liam staring worriedly at Lorenzo. "What are you going to do?"

"Pay a friend a visit. Send me his address."

Liam placed a hand on Lorenzo's arm. "It might not be the obvious explanation. He let me and Shaun go in Blackpool. Listen to what he has to say."

Grimly, Lorenzo nodded.

* * * *

An hour later, Lorenzo found himself outside a little terraced house. Rows of identical buildings stood testament to Manchester's industrial past. It was a decent enough street. Jonny had always insisted his lads didn't have showy houses. It would attract suspicion.

Of course, he allowed himself to have a mansion with a pool and all the mod cons. *Good old Jonny, treating everyone fairly as usual.*

Lorenzo looked around him. *So this is where Harry calls home.* Back in the day, they had moved from one flat to the other, each one an improvement on the last as the money rolled in.

His heart raced as he took it all in. The hanging baskets, the expensive curtains and the neatly tended garden at the front. This was Harry's world. In another life, it could have been theirs.

Swallowing hard, he knocked on the door, the thoughts of alternative futures shoved to a far corner of his mind. Now he had to see just where Harry stood. Once and for all.

He heard movement inside. At least Harry was in. This grand gesture would have been pointless if they'd got to him first. The net curtains moved and there was the face of Harry. When he saw who stood on his doorstep, he scurried to the door and yanked it open. "What the fuck are you doing?"

"We need to talk."

"Get inside."

Harry dragged him over the threshold. He glanced up and down the street before he closed the door. "How did you get my address?"

"How do you think?"

"Liam. Jesus, Lorenzo, are you trying to get us both killed? Go through into the back."

Lorenzo walked through the small house. It was immaculate. Harry always did have good taste. Even when he'd had a crappy flat, he covered the damp patches with art prints and posters of local bands.

Now he had money, he had filled his little house with gorgeous paintings and expensive furniture. Anyone else in this area would have been burgled long ago. It would be a fool who went for Wellingham's right-hand man.

The dining room gave them privacy from the road. Even so, Harry drew the curtains. Prying eyes could be anywhere in these streets.

"Sit down," Harry said.

"No thanks," Lorenzo replied. He studied Harry's face for any sign of nerves. All he found there was confusion.

"What are you doing here?"

Lorenzo took hold of Harry's hand. He stared deep into his eyes. "Is there anything you need to tell me? Anything that if I found out could ruin everything. Between us, I mean. This is really important, Harry. Now is the time."

"What like? Lorenzo, I don't know what you mean."

"Because if I had any suspicion you'd been playing me... Well, I can't be responsible for what could happen."

"Lorenzo, you're scaring me. What's going on?"

Letting Harry's hand drop, Lorenzo paced the room. He wanted to believe him so badly. Every cell in his body yearned for his words to be true. Perhaps he should have brought Liam. Indecision plagued Lorenzo about what to do for the best. "Have you spoken to Jonny today?"

"Of course. He's in Lincoln for a few days. He's taken Sadie to her mother's. I think he's expecting trouble and he's not risking her again. Is he right? Is there bother coming?"

Lorenzo had questioned people before. A lot of the time it involved questionable means. Even so, he could see the signs of a lie at fifty paces. Unable to maintain eye contact, overreaction or wild theories to throw him off the scent. None of it was present in Harry's little dining room.

He decided to gamble. "Someone at the farm is giving Jonny information."

"What?"

"You heard me."

Harry's face told him everything he needed to know. He had absolutely no idea. Lorenzo wanted to kiss him furiously. Instead, he watched helplessly as Harry sank down on a chair. "Jonny wouldn't set something like that up without telling me. He absolutely wouldn't."

That was the piece of the jigsaw that just didn't fit. Why hadn't Jonny told Harry?

"Looks like you don't know everything," Lorenzo said, sitting at the chair next to him. "Think. We need to find out who it is and fast."

Shaking his head, Harry seemed lost in thought. "Lorenzo, I have absolutely no idea. Are you sure?"

Lorenzo nodded. "Jonny wasn't taking his spawn to safety. He stole our consignment last night. The only way he could have known where it was is from the inside."

Harry's eyes widened. "When did this happen? I don't know anything about it. Is this a trick? Because if it is, this is bullshit, Lorenzo."

"Why would I want to trick you?"

"I don't know. To get me to join you perhaps?" Harry asked.

Lorenzo shrugged. "I do want that. Only if you do, of course. I'm not going to force you. Although, I'm sorry my love, I think that decision might be made."

"I didn't know about this. I promise you."

Harry went to get up. Lorenzo took hold of his hands. They were shaking. Lorenzo refused to believe this to be an elaborate bluff. No one could act that well.

"Wait. Stop. I believe you," Lorenzo said. "We need to accept the fact that Jonny hasn't told you means he's onto you. Or us, I should say."

The realisation dawned on Harry, and he clutched Lorenzo's hand harder. "How can he be? We've been so careful."

"Not from someone feeding him information. I haven't broadcast it to anyone. Gab was at the hotel with us last night. Plus, Tommasso and Fed both knew it. All it would take would be eyes on the hotel to see you coming in."

Harry looked as if he were about to throw up. "Then why hasn't he put a bullet in me?"

"Think about it properly," Lorenzo urged. "You're more useful to him alive at the moment. I'm sure he has plans for you further down the line. The fucker isn't happy turning one of my nephews against me. He's probably thinking about feeding you all sorts of shit to tell me."

Clutching his hands, Harry stared at Lorenzo. "I had no idea. Tell me again that you believe me."

Lorenzo might be being totally irrational. His instincts told him that Harry was on the level and anyone who disagreed could go fuck themselves. "I believe you. You can't stay here. It isn't safe. The minute Wellingham suspects we know what he's up to, he'll kill you. Chances are he's got the house on watch."

"Then why did you bloody come here?"

"I can hardly make an appointment with you, can I? You need to run and I'll take you somewhere safe."

Harry scrubbed his face with shaking hands. He stared around his little home, his eyes filling with tears. Lorenzo wanted to go to him, but he had to let the thoughts form by themselves. He just wished they would get on with it.

They both leapt sky high as Harry's phone rang. Glancing at the display, Harry swallowed. "It's him."

"Answer it. Act natural."

Harry pressed a button. "Jon? You home from dropping Sadie off? You were quick."

Lorenzo could barely contain his rage as he heard the muffled voice of Wellingham. How he would like to grab that phone from Harry and scream every threat in the world. To give Jonny credit, he had them in a trap. That rankled with Lorenzo worse than anything.

"Right," Harry said. "Where is it? Okay, okay. I doubt he's tapping the phones. Okay, Jon, have it your way. I'll be ready." He terminated the call.

"What did he want?" Lorenzo asked.

"They're moving the gang. A new place. He's sending two of the lads round to pick me up."

"Did he say where?"

Harry shook his head. "He reckons he doesn't trust the phones."

"What a crock of shit. I'm not bloody James Bond. I can't bug a whole mobile network," Lorenzo muttered. "Right, grab whatever you want to take. Anything with sentimental value. Quickly."

Harry dithered for a second. His endless thinking used to drive Lorenzo mad and it still did.

"Wait, this is my home."

"And it will be your fucking tomb if you hang around. I'll send one of the lads down when this is over. You know, to rescue anything. It's time to jump, Harry. Just be fucking grateful I'm here to catch you."

Harry nodded and dashed upstairs. While he packed, Lorenzo tried to take in what was happening. Had he been so blinded by his affair with Harry that he'd given Jonny the chance to pull this masterstroke? He felt furious with himself. With shaking fingers, he placed a call to Liam. "What's happening?"

"I could say the same to you," Liam replied. "The stock is on the move."

Lorenzo relaxed a little. Gary Brooks would be pissed that Wellingham had intercepted the new stuff. At least Lorenzo could placate him by selling the existing stuff while they waited for more.

"Meet me at the flat," Lorenzo said. "I'm getting him out of here. Wellingham is onto us."

"Are you sure?" Liam asked.

"I am."

"Fine," Liam said. "I'll be there."

Just the two words from Lorenzo and Liam was on board. He clearly trusted Lorenzo implicitly and he barely even knew him. Marco would have argued until the sun set about the merits of dumping Harry's body in the canal.

Harry half ran, half fell down the stairs clutching two suitcases. "Everything else can go up in smoke." he panted. "It's amazing how little any of it means when it comes down to it."

"Very philosophical. Now move," Lorenzo said, almost pushing Harry out of the door.

Thankfully, the long straight road was empty.

"Wait," Harry said, rummaging in his pocket. He got out his phone and threw it into the hallway before slamming the door. "I'm on my own now."

Lorenzo kissed him hard. "No, you're not."

They got into Lorenzo's car and he floored it. The exhilaration at having Harry by his side, out and proud, exploded with him as he drove out of the quiet little street.

"Where are we going?" Harry asked.

"Town," Lorenzo replied. "Liam is meeting us at a flat."

"Liam? Are you sure about this?"

"I trust him with my life."

"What about with mine?"

Mercifully, traffic wasn't too bad in the centre of Manchester. Lorenzo was a bit rusty with navigating these streets. With Harry giving him instructions, it felt like old times.

"You have a flat in there?" Harry said, staring up at the huge skyscraper that had dominated the Manchester skyline for decades. "We should have known when Marco stashed his stuff there. Fuck that seems like a lifetime ago."

Lorenzo grabbed him by the arm. "Cut the 'we'. I don't like it."

Harry pulled himself free. "You can't expect me to erase the last twenty years of my life. Give me a fucking break, okay? It's been a shit day."

Lorenzo instantly regretted his words. The anxiety of getting Harry to safety had clouded his judgement. He hadn't stopped to think how Harry must be feeling, having to leave his home and life. "I'm sorry," he said. "I just hate that bastard."

"Me too," Harry replied. "We can't fall out. Otherwise, it's all been for nothing."

They walked into the building and straight to the lifts. The concierge barely looked up. *So much for security.*

Inside the safety of the lift, Harry visibly relaxed. "I can't believe I'm here with you."

Lorenzo held him close. "If you'd listened to me in the first place, we wouldn't have had all this drama."

Harry pouted. "If you hadn't played dead for fifteen years, we could be sunbathing in Tuscany now."

He had Lorenzo there. Thankfully, the lift reached its destination, and they scurried down the corridor. Lorenzo half expected one of Jonny's goons to jump out of a neighbouring apartment toting a gun.

He knocked hard on the door of their flat. Liam opened it. He was a sight for sore eyes.

"Liam," Harry said.

"Harry."

Lorenzo couldn't decipher the look between them. They had a shared history that stretched back a decade. He hadn't stopped to think what it would be like for them to be on the same side again. They had such a lot to discuss. "Let's get in," Lorenzo said, glancing over his shoulder.

They all walked through the narrow hallway and into the lounge and kitchen area. The floor-to-ceiling windows gave a spectacular view of the city. But it wasn't that which took Lorenzo's breath away.

On the sofa sat an angry Marco.

Chapter Fourteen

"Marco—"

"I'm sorry, Lorenzo," Liam cut in. "He wouldn't let me leave without my telling him where I was going. I won't lie to him. You can't expect it."

Marco stood, trembling. "That you even asked Liam to keep something from me is totally out of order. Then to see you two walking in here like everything is normal? What the fuck do you think you're doing?"

Three of the most important people in Lorenzo's life were in one room and they could quite easily tear one another to pieces.

Fuck you, Jonny Wellingham. You will not do this to me.

"Shall we all just sit down?" Lorenzo asked.

"This is your fucking lover?" Marco replied. "This piece of shit?"

Liam crossed the room and laid a hand on Marco's shoulder. "You need to listen, Marco. Please."

Fear gripped Lorenzo. The betrayal that was written all over Marco's face cut him deep. However, the relief at things being out in the open couldn't be denied. He had to get through to his nephew that his feelings were real. That he had Harry all wrong. Not so easy when he was missing a tooth and a lot of self-respect.

"I understand why you are upset," Lorenzo said. "Liam, Harry, can you give us a minute?"

Liam glanced at Marco, who nodded miserably, the initial maelstrom of anger having passed. It was always the way with his nephew, a huge explosion, then calm.

Liam led Harry into the bedroom. As he left the room, Harry looked at Lorenzo. What Lorenzo read in those eyes was hope. It spurred him on. If he expected Harry to jump into unknown territory, he had to do the same. "Sit," he instructed.

Marco sank onto the sofa. Tears were pouring down his cheeks. "I trusted everything you said."

Lorenzo sat next to him and rested his hand on his knee. "You're spinning and that's fine. It's still me, little one."

"Don't you 'little one' me."

"Marco, look at me. It's true, Harry is my lover. I should have told you. How could I with everything else that is going on?"

"Because I'm your fucking nephew. I tell you everything."

Lorenzo raised an eyebrow. "Hardly. We don't need to go into the many times you've gone off on your own then asked me to fix it. You also can't lecture me on sleeping with the enemy."

"That's different."

Lorenzo would take this insolence to a point. Marco had to remember who he was talking to. "There is no difference whatsoever. Apart from the fact that Harry and I have history. Imagine if I had told you to walk away from Liam when I got here. That I had decided it too dangerous to have a Wellingham Boy in our midst? What would you have done?"

Marco played with the toggle on his hoodie. He couldn't meet his uncle's gaze. "I would have told you to stick it."

"There," Lorenzo said. "The difference is, I never asked that of you. Not once. I accepted Liam into our family without question."

"Taking a bullet for me might have had something to do with it," Marco muttered.

"Do you want me to shoot Harry to prove to you his feelings for me? Don't be so ridiculous. I think you'll find I was willing to protect Liam long before that. It was you, acting hastily as usual, who caused that bullet."

Marco began to say something and thought better of it.

"Now will you hear me out?" Lorenzo continued.

Marco nodded. "Fine."

Lorenzo settled on the couch. Only silence came from the bedroom. Harry and Liam were probably listening to every word. "Harry and I were together when I was shot," he began. "Had been for a good while. When I came back here, I knew I would have to see him. I didn't expect my feelings to be exactly the same the minute I laid eyes on him."

To his credit, Marco was listening.

"You know as well as I do that these things can't be controlled," Lorenzo continued. For a man used to having his every wish dealt with, to be pleading a case came as an unusual experience. Not one he had any intention of getting used to.

"When were you going to tell me?"

"I spoke to Liam to help me to do it. It's just that things have overtaken us. I never wanted you to find out like this. However, now that you do know, hear me, Harry is going nowhere. I'm in love with him, Marco."

Marco put his head in his hands. "Why him? Jesus Christ."

"Is it so hard to believe? It happens all the time. Enzo and Shaun, you and Liam. We deal with so much shit, to want to find love is only natural."

Marco stared into his eyes. "And you love him?"

Lorenzo nodded and he hoped desperately that Harry heard these words too. "More than anything in the world. You have to accept this, Marco. I know it won't happen immediately. We can't let Wellingham derail us like this. There are bigger problems that we must face as a united front. Otherwise, we may as well head home to Roma and leave this city to Wellingham again. I don't think you want that and I bloody well know I don't."

He glanced again at the city. Lorenzo had wanted control of this city since long before Jonny had even made his move. Even in the early days, he'd fantasised about him and Harry being the ones who called the shots. Jonny had the money and contacts in those days, but things were very different now.

Shrugging, Marco wiped a tear from his eye. "I won't cause trouble. I don't like it and I don't like him, but I won't cause trouble."

Lorenzo felt so proud of his nephew at that moment. For the first time he had controlled his anger and could see what had to be done. He had learnt a difficult lesson. One that would make him a solid leader one day. "Can I ask them to come in without you flying off the handle?"

Marco nodded.

"Liam. Harry."

Liam came in first. He sat next to Marco and took his hand. Marco nuzzled into his shoulder. A pensive Harry stood in the doorway. Lorenzo thought it best that they weren't all over each other. This was only the first step on a very long journey.

"Before you ask," Lorenzo said, "Harry has no idea about this mole."

Marco laughed. "And we're expected to believe that?"

Lorenzo banged his hand down on the coffee table, making them all jump. "Yes, you bloody well are. Don't get above yourself, Marco."

He noticed Liam grasping Marco's hand. His nephew would do well to allow his lover to calm him.

"Marco, I know you hate me, and I don't blame you," Harry said, edging into the room. "Jonny kept the mole and the hijack from me. We think he was onto us."

"Who the hell is it?" Liam asked. "How do we find out?"

"Fuck knows," Harry replied. "You and I both know that Jonny will be loving this chaos."

Liam nodded.

"There must be a way," Lorenzo said. "Do I just send all three home?"

"That's cutting off our nose to spite our face," Liam replied. "We can't lose two for the sake of one."

He had a point. Lorenzo did not want to have to force a confession out of one of them. To do that to one of his nephews was inconceivable.

"We flush them out," Marco said quietly.

"What do you mean?" Lorenzo asked.

Marco looked at each of them in turn. "We give them each a false location for the existing stock, of course. Liam and I will go and move it to a completely different place."

It could work. "Won't they talk to each other?" Lorenzo said.

"Not if you tell them they're the only ones who know," Harry said. "The two loyal will remain loyal and the mole will want to get closer to you. It's a good idea, Marco."

"Thanks." Marco sneered.

Lorenzo decided to let that tone slide. Marco needed to understand, he wouldn't have too many chances like that.

"I don't like all this stock moving," Liam said. "It increases our chances of getting picked up by the bloody coppers. We don't need that on top of everything else."

"Agreed. We have no choice at this point," Lorenzo said. "From now on, only us four know where stock is to be held."

Marco glared at Harry. Whatever dark thoughts he was thinking, he mercifully kept to himself. Instead he looked to Liam. "Where?"

"Why not here?" Liam suggested.

It was perfect. Lorenzo wished he'd come up with it. "And the fake locations?"

"Leave them to us," Liam said, getting to his feet. "I know plenty of places. If Wellingham turns up, we'll know about it."

He held out his hand for Marco, who took and hauled himself up.

"Can you handle it?" Lorenzo asked.

"Of course. It was my idea, wasn't it?"

Marco led Liam towards the door.

"Marco?" Lorenzo called after him. "You've impressed me today."

Marco glanced at Harry then back at Lorenzo before silently walking out.

Once they were alone, Lorenzo let out a huge sigh of relief.

"Fuck," Harry said.

"Fuck indeed," Lorenzo said.

He got up off the chair and went to Harry, putting his arms around him, the scent of Harry enough to calm him. "Come," he said, gently tugging Harry towards his bedroom.

Once inside, Harry began to say something. Lorenzo silenced him with his lips. He had finished with talking. He wanted to feel. "Prove to me everything I've done is going to be worth it," he dared.

Harry kissed him hard, biting at his lower lip, his hands holding Lorenzo's head. Almost as if he wanted to be possessed by him.

They paused only to get their clothes off. Naked, they collapsed onto the bed. Lorenzo felt Harry everywhere as he wrapped his body around him, his hard abs rubbing against Lorenzo's cock as Harry bit and played with his nipples. He sent shockwaves up his spine to the base of his neck.

"Oh, God, Harry."

Quick as a flash, Harry shifted down and took Lorenzo's cock fully in his mouth. Lorenzo hadn't been expecting that and writhed as he surfed the wave of pleasure overwhelming his body.

Lorenzo gazed down at him, gorging on his dick. Sucking greedily, Harry massaged his balls at the same time. Lorenzo bucked his hips, fucking Harry's mouth.

Before he could pass a point of no return, Harry crawled up his body and they kissed hard. Rolling over, Lorenzo positioned himself between Harry's legs, his cock rubbing against his balls.

Harry gripped his arse cheeks as he ground himself against him.

"Fuck me," Harry begged.

Lorenzo sat on his heels, leaning over to his jacket to grab condoms and lube. When he glanced back at Harry, he had one arm behind his head and the other hand slowly stroking his cock.

His heart leapt. He needed Harry. Possibly more than he'd ever needed anything in his life. Jonny had done them a favour. Now they could be together, no matter what.

Running the lube over his fingers, he stared into Harry's eyes. Their shared knowledge of what would follow was more of a turn-on than those sexy first times.

He stroked Harry's hole, teasing the rim. Harry gasped and pushed down a little. Circling with his finger, he gently pressed. At first, Harry's body fought him, but Lorenzo made his way inside, coating the edge with the lube.

"More," Harry murmured.

Lorenzo slid his finger inside. God, it felt good. Harry matched his movement with groans. Lorenzo added another finger, massaging Harry's prostate and making him squirm.

With his free hand, he deftly rolled a condom on to his own cock. Then, when he knew Harry was ready, he slid his fingers out and pressed his dick against the hole.

Harry lifted his legs onto Lorenzo's shoulders.

Lorenzo kissed his calf. "I love you, Harry. There's nothing else I can say."

"I love you too," Harry replied.

Then he cried out in pleasure as Lorenzo's cock entered him. The passion that had consumed them earlier burnt into Lorenzo. The heat coming from Harry had sparked it.

He started to fuck him, hard. Harry grasped the sheets at the sudden increase in tempo. "Oh, fuck yeah, Lorenzo."

Holding Harry's ankles, Lorenzo dove in and out of him. Unable to contain himself, he leant forward and kissed Harry. Still fucking him hard, he thrust his tongue in Harry's mouth. He needed to connect with him in every way possible.

Harry had wrapped his legs around Lorenzo's waist and held on to him by the back of his neck. The bed shook as he fucked him. Then he couldn't wait much longer. He pulled out. "Get on your hands and knees," he panted.

Harry changed positions, leaning down so Lorenzo saw his perfect hole. He ran his hand over Harry's butt cheek. He could fuck him forever.

Pushing his cock inside Harry once more, he gripped his hips and fucked him. Harry yanked at his own cock with one hand and steadied them against the headboard with the other.

"Come on, Lorenzo," he grunted. "Come for me."

Sweat poured from Lorenzo's forehead as he fucked all the worries away. He craved that moment of obliteration and became solely focused on getting it.

"Oh fuck," Harry stammered. "I'm coming."

His arse muscles contracted around Lorenzo's cock, triggering his own orgasm to explode from him.

Digging his fingers into Harry's flesh, he arched his body. Release rushed through his system as he let the spasms rock him.

Aftershock followed aftershock. Eventually he got himself together enough to pull out of Harry. Throwing the condom into the bin, he flopped down next to Harry, who lay flat on his back and panting.

They lay in silence. The only sound Lorenzo could hear was his own heartbeat. He felt Harry's little finger become entwined with his own, and the rush of connection made him almost drunk.

"I do love you," Harry whispered.

"And I you," Lorenzo replied. "Now all we have to do is to stay alive to enjoy it."

Chapter Fifteen

As much as he would have liked to lie in bed with Harry all day and pretend the rest of it wasn't happening, Liam and Marco would return at some point. Walking in to find them buck-naked would push Marco too far.

By the time Lorenzo got out of the shower, Harry was dressed and staring out of the window. Lorenzo hastily threw on a pair of jeans and a shirt before joining him.

The city of Manchester lay below them, a place that had haunted Lorenzo's worst nightmares. Now he was so close to ruling it. His papa would be proud.

"What are you thinking?" Lorenzo asked, drying his curly hair with a towel.

"How I'd be happy to never set eyes on this place again."

Lorenzo threw the towel down and came up behind him. Kissing the back of his neck, he marvelled at them being together. "We finish what I started. Then we run.

You and me and the Tuscan sun. How does that sound?"

Harry took hold of his hand and kissed it. "Like heaven."

Lorenzo rested his head on Harry's shoulder. Manchester had been the stage for some of the most important moments in his life. He was absolutely determined he would leave on a high.

The door opening disturbed their moment of peace. They sprang away from each other. Marco and Liam were laden down with supermarket shopping bags as they struggled in.

"Here." Lorenzo took one of the bags from Liam. "We'll put them in the wardrobes. Come."

He noticed Marco awkwardly hand one bag over to Harry. That had to be progress. They stashed the bags in the wardrobe.

"How many more?" Lorenzo asked.

"Another load," Marco replied. "Come on, Li."

"I'll come with you," Lorenzo butted in.

Marco glanced at Liam who nodded. Shrugging, Marco ushered Lorenzo the way they had come. "You're the boss."

Lorenzo bit back the temptation to tell Marco not to forget that. The shaky foundations they appeared to have built did not need any extra stress. What Lorenzo planned to say in the lift might shatter them completely.

He followed Marco down the corridor. At the end, Marco pressed the button.

"You okay?" Lorenzo asked.

"I guess," Marco replied. "And before you say it, it's not about Harry. It's about the guys. One of them is putting us in danger. Why?"

That question that had been playing on Lorenzo's mind too. Why would a member of his own family turn on him like that? It couldn't be money. He was more than generous. There had to be something else. "I guess time will tell," he replied.

The lift came and they stepped in. Once inside the confines of the metal box, Lorenzo felt safer from people overhearing. "I need to say something," he began. "I'm not comfortable with Harry staying at the flat. There's tens of thousands of pounds of drugs in there."

Marco whirled around. "You'd better not be about to say what I think you are."

"Which is?"

"That you want to bring him to the farm."

"I don't want him out of my sight, Marco. Can't you understand that?"

"Sure, and will you be moving into Giovanni's old room so he can remember shooting them?"

Fury overtook Lorenzo and he shoved his nephew up against the lift wall. "He had nothing to do with that. Do you think I would be sleeping with the man who killed your cousin?"

Marco roughly pulled himself free. "But I bet he knew about it."

"Of course, he fucking did. Think about this business, Marco. Are you telling me you're squeaky clean? You dragged Liam's brother into this life as well as Dolly and Claire. You knew how big the stakes were. You made out like you were just exploring business opportunities. You have just as much blood on your hands as Harry. Don't you forget that."

They reached the basement. Marco bolted out of the lift. Lorenzo followed him over to the SUV. He made sure to keep his head down. Cameras were everywhere.

"The lads will go berserk," Marco muttered as he opened the boot.

Inside were six more bags. Lorenzo was pleased to see Marco had scattered a layer of vegetables over the top. Even with the most sophisticated CCTV system, it would look like they were innocently unloading shopping.

He took three of the bags. Marco grabbed the others.

"You'll support me when I tell them," Lorenzo grunted as they walked to the lift.

"Fine." Marco sighed. "I'll tell you this, Uncle. The first sign of danger to you, Liam or anyone in that building, I shoot him. Is that clear?"

Lorenzo smiled. The ferocity with which Marco defended the operation couldn't be faulted. He couldn't buy that kind of loyalty, even if it was getting right in his way at that moment. "I love you, little one."

Marco's eyes filled with tears. "I love you too, Uncle Z. Why did you have to fall for him?"

"I think it's a bit like Romeo and Juliet."

The lift arrived and they stepped in.

"And look what happened to them." Marco pressed the button.

As the lift doors closed, they both sighed.

"What a fucking life this is," Lorenzo said.

"You're not wrong," Marco agreed. "I'll send two of the lads down here tonight to keep an eye on things. I'm sure they'll take the risk to spend time in a luxury apartment and not a campervan. I will tell them it's top secret. The Three Musketeers won't find out."

Lorenzo appraised his nephew. "One step ahead of me again, little one. I will have to watch my back."

* * * *

A sea of eyes was trained on him. Once again, Lorenzo found himself out of his comfort zone. This had become an alarming habit.

He cleared his throat. Marco, to his credit, wasn't scowling. Lorenzo decided to mark that as an improvement. The only kind face he found was Liam. The rest of the lads were staring at him agog.

"You're shagging Jonny Wellingham's right-hand man?" Tommasso asked.

"If he's Jonny's right hand, are you technically getting wanked off by Jonny?" one of the other lads piped up.

Lorenzo threw an apple at him. "Next time I'll hit you where you won't ever get wanked off again,"

The joke had lightened the mood. Everyone shifted uneasily as a lull fell over the room once more.

"You didn't answer my question," Tommasso said. "What is the point of all this if you're fucking the enemy?"

The atmosphere dropped. No one had ever dared speak to Lorenzo like that before. *Here comes the test.*

"Your questions are offensive, Tommasso. Who I fuck is my business. The point of this is to regain Manchester and take Wellingham down. You don't think turning his prime asset a blow to him?"

Tommasso seemed lost for words.

"We all play our parts, gentlemen," Lorenzo said. "It's true, some are more dispensable than others. We are all needed regardless. Jonny will be wounded by this treachery in the same way I would be if I ever found out one of you was feeding him information."

He noticed Liam and Marco scanning the room. They had pre-arranged this in the car up here.

"So, you will understand that Harry is in a difficult predicament. That's why we're going to give him shelter here."

A gasp rippled through the crowd. Gabriel raised his hand.

"Yes, Gab."

"Can I ask you something personal, boss?"

"You can ask. I might not answer."

"Are you one hundred percent about Harry? Not one tiny percent of doubt?"

It was a totally fair question and one he could answer honestly. "Not even a fraction of a percent, Gabriel."

Gabriel shrugged. "That's enough for me. Try to keep the noise down at night, yeah? It's bad enough having to listen to those two."

"Fuck off," Marco shouted, laughing.

"Is he outside?" Fed asked. Lorenzo nodded. "Then you'd better bring him in. He'll be freezing his balls off."

Liam dashed off. A wave of anxiety swept over Lorenzo. Could it be this easy? In no time, Liam led Harry into the room. He looked absolutely terrified.

"Gentlemen," he said, nodding. "I know I'm not welcome here, and I fully understand why. I won't take the piss. I'll keep out of the way. Thank you. I truly mean that."

Harry had insisted on this. He fully recognised to have him lazing on the sofas or waiting at the dining table for dinner would be disrespectful. He would stay in Lorenzo's room for the foreseeable while things settled.

Lorenzo led Harry up the stairs and into his room. It was pretty grim, like the rest of the farm. It remained in stark contrast to Harry's lovely little home that they'd left vulnerable to Jonny's vengeful ways.

Harry sat on the edge of the bed. "Well, that went well."

Lorenzo ran his hands over Harry's head and drew him close. "It'll be fine. They're good lads on the whole."

Lowering himself so he straddled Harry, Lorenzo kissed his forehead. "If you're a prisoner in this room, it seems only fair that I stay with you as much as possible."

Harry ran his hands over Lorenzo's butt, thumbing his waistband and sending chills up Lorenzo's spine. "Two people trapped in a room. It's quite horny."

Harry lay on the bed, pulling Lorenzo down on top of him. Lorenzo kissed him lightly, their lips barely brushing. He could smell Harry's scent, fresh and manly, the same as it had ever been.

"Is it wrong to be happy amidst all this?" Harry asked.

Grinning, Lorenzo kissed the tip of his nose. "Well, if it's wrong, I don't want to be right."

Harry groaned and pushed Lorenzo onto his back. "That's bad, Lorenzo. Jesus, what idiots have you been bedding who fall for shit like that?"

"Hey, my moves are legendary."

"And very dated, my love. Good job you don't need them anymore."

Lorenzo grabbed Harry into a hug. This was more than he'd ever dared hope for. Even if Jonny Wellingham killed him the next day, nothing could quell the happiness in Lorenzo's heart right at that moment.

"You know what would help get you in with the lads properly?"

"I'm not cooking."

Lorenzo raised his head and rested his chin on Harry's chest. "I'm serious. If you took a more active role, giving us an insight…they would appreciate that."

"You'd appreciate it too, I suppose."

"I would be so appreciative. You'd be amazed."

Harry stared up at the ceiling. "I'll do it, Lorenzo. For all the reasons you've mentioned. Mostly because I want us to be free. I have one requirement."

"Name it."

"You won't like it."

"Name it, I said."

"He survives."

Lorenzo sprang up. "What? Are you being serious? How much more am I supposed to deal with today? Of course he can't survive. Why are you trying to save his saggy arse?"

Harry grabbed hold of his hands and led him onto the bed. "I'm not saving him, you fuckwit. I'm saving *us*. What kind of life can we have if you're on the run for his murder? He'd be winning then."

Lorenzo hadn't really thought past putting a bullet in Wellingham. He hadn't dared when he and Harry were apart. Now they were together properly, that changed things. "I'm not agreeing to this. I'll hear out any plan that you have. That will have to be enough."

"That's all I ask for."

Lorenzo kissed him. "You can ask anything you like from me. I'm so glad to have you in my lair. Now I can keep you safe and nothing will hurt you again."

"Don't make promises you can't keep, Lorenzo," Harry said. "We both know Jonny will be fucking raging."

Lorenzo took Harry's hand and guided it to his groin. "Say it again, baby. You're making me hard."

Harry laughed. "Jonny will be so angry he will be smashing the place up."

"Oh yeah, tell me about his face. How red is he?"

Before Harry could tell him, there came a frantic knock at the door. They both rearranged themselves and sat bolt upright on the bed like a couple in a fifties sitcom.

"Yes?" Lorenzo called out as innocently as possible...which wasn't all that convincing.

Marco stuck his head around the door. "Wellingham is on the move."

"What?" Lorenzo said. "Already? Jesus Christ, the leak is more of a bloody flood. Shall I come down?"

Marco shook his head. "No need. I'll tell you as soon as I hear where he's headed."

Lorenzo nodded grimly. "Fuck," he exclaimed after Marco had closed the door behind him. "Everyone is in the farm tonight. It's like some fucked-up game show."

He got up and walked over to the window. It was a cloudless night, the moon shining down on the frosty fields. A member of his own family betraying them ranked as one of the worst feelings in the world. How would he tell his brother or sister, depending on who became unmasked?

The bigger question was how he would deal with it. He had dealt with spies in the camp before and brutally. *Never family.* There would have to be another way.

"You look like you have the weight of the world on your shoulders," Harry said softly.

Lorenzo turned. The warm lamp light falling on Harry made his heart explode. It felt so right to be here with him now.

"I love you," Lorenzo said. "I'm going to get us out of this, and we'll live the quiet life. We can travel and do everything we've ever dreamt of. Marco and Liam can take over here and there's plenty in Roma chomping at the bit for my seat."

"Do you mean it? You wouldn't miss all this?"

"Pah." Lorenzo jumped onto the bed. "The last fifteen years have been working up to this moment. After this, everything else will be dull. No, I'll quit while I'm ahead and I claim you as my prize."

Harry kissed him. "Then we'll neutralise Jonny Wellingham. Give me some time and I'll come up with something. Please?"

"Fine," Lorenzo said. "I have problems closer to home anyway."

Footsteps thundered up the stairs.

"I think that might be about to be revealed," Harry said.

"Jesus, it's fast-paced tonight."

Lorenzo winced when someone hammered on the door as though they had the devil after them. "Come in," he shouted.

Both Liam and Marco almost fell through the door, panting.

"Get in," Lorenzo urged. "You're being about as stealthy as a rhinoceros."

Once inside, Marco swallowed hard. "It's Tommasso."

Chapter Sixteen

Lorenzo watched Tommasso helping himself to coffee like he didn't have a care in the world. The rest of the lads busied themselves around, getting their breakfast and making jokes.

If only they knew.

After Marco had broken the news, the temptation to rip Tommasso's head off was great. Harry had stayed him with his calming hands and soft voice. The four of them had talked long into the night about what to do.

Eventually, Marco had suggested they keep it between them. Tommasso could be useful. If he suspected they were onto him, he would just run. Lorenzo didn't fancy Tommasso's chances of survival with Jonny once he stopped being useful. No matter what, Tommasso had to survive.

"Tommasso," Lorenzo barked.

Tommasso whirled around, a flash of panic on his face. "Yes, boss?"

"I fancy croissants for breakfast. Can you go and find us some, please?"

Tommasso frowned. It was a lowly job that Lorenzo would usually give to one of the other lads. "Me?"

"Yes, you," Lorenzo replied. "Do you have a problem with that?"

Tommasso took a sip of his coffee. "No, course not."

Without catching anyone's eye, Tommasso grabbed his coat and left the room. Lorenzo glared after him. "Get Gab and Fed. We're having a meeting."

Marco scurried off to find his cousins, leaving only Lorenzo and Liam at the table.

"What are you going to do?"

"Oh, fuck knows," Lorenzo said. All of a sudden, fatigue overcame him. "I came here to wreak my revenge. It's getting so fucking complicated now. Harry, him, everything."

Liam smiled. "Not what you expected then?"

It was a shrewd question. Lorenzo didn't really know what he'd expected it would be like coming back. Of course, he'd fantasised about Jonny's face when Lorenzo finally got the better of him. Harry's words from the night before still rang in his ears.

"For the last fifteen years, I've been totally carefree," he explained. "If I was jailed or killed, what did it matter? I wasn't really living. Now it's totally different. I have a future to worry about."

Frowning, Liam stared at him. "I don't understand. Surely, you're not giving up."

"No, not that. Harry wants me to do it without killing him. But…"

"You're not so sure?"

"That man is scum. The world would be a better place without him in it. I don't know if I can be strong enough to walk away from him."

"What are you going to do?"

Lorenzo shook his head. "I've said I'll listen to any ideas that Harry may have. I can't say fairer than that, can I?"

The others started to come in. Liam leant forward. "Welcome to the world of relationships," he whispered. "It's shit."

Marco led the other two into the kitchen. Most of the lads were out in the campervans or on guard duty.

"Shut the door," Lorenzo said. "I want to talk to you, confidentially."

Fed and Gab sat at the table, worry etched over their faces.

"What is it?" Fed asked.

"I've got to say something to you and it's not going to be easy to hear. Someone is leaking information to Jonny."

Both of them sat back as if stung.

"No fucking way," Gabriel muttered. "Who? I'll rip their balls off."

Lorenzo glanced at Marco, who nodded. Fuck, this was hard. He returned his gaze to Gab. "It's your brother," he said as gently as he could.

"I can't believe it," Gabriel countered. "He wouldn't."

"It's true, Gab," Marco said. "Remember me telling you about the new place for what stock we've got left?"

Gabriel nodded.

"We gave you all a different location," Liam continued. "Jonny raided the place we told Tommasso."

Hanging his head, Gabriel let out a sob. Fed, on the other hand, looked stone-faced.

"Fed?" Lorenzo said.

"Before I say anything, I want your assurance you won't kill him."

Lorenzo exhaled. "I haven't decided what I'm going to do yet. If you have any information, I strongly suggest you share it."

Fed fiddled with a stray knife that had been left on the table. "I won't sign my own brother's death warrant, Uncle."

Lorenzo could hardly believe they were having this conversation. Had he really resorted to grilling one nephew so he could build a case against another? "Of course I won't kill him," he fired back. "You're my blood. Jonny Wellingham has made me do some terrible things. I will not let him lead me down that road."

All four men around the table visibly relaxed.

"That's a relief," Marco said. "When did you decide that?"

"When three men who I still see as little boys sat in front of me," Lorenzo said, gesturing to them. "I bottle-fed all of you. I want to understand what's made him do this."

Fed swallowed. "He's seeing a woman. I don't know who, before you ask. He's been sneaking off. He was bragging that he's the only one of us getting it."

That sounded like Tommasso. So, Jonny had set a honey trap, had he? *Typical of Tommasso to fall for it as well. He's never been the brightest.*

"Okay, I'll guarantee his safety. But we can't let him know we're onto him," Lorenzo said. "If he runs, he's dead. Jonny will have filled his head of all sorts of bullshit. Fed, you'll be responsible for dripping the info to him. He speaks to you. Gab, I want a tracker in his car. Go into Manchester and get one."

They both nodded and got up. As they were leaving, Gabriel turned. "Thank you for sparing him, Uncle. I know it won't go down well."

"This stays between us," Lorenzo said. "Forever. You got that?"

After they had gone, Lorenzo caught Marco watching him intently. "And how may I help you, little one?"

"I thought going against the family like that was punishable by death. What's changed?"

Lorenzo looked up to the ceiling. "There is a man up there who is teaching me a different point of view. He's just saved your cousin's life."

* * * *

The day was a busy one. Lorenzo, Marco and Liam had gone into town to meet with Greg Brooks. Then, they'd checked the stock. Everything was still intact. The weekend loomed and Manchester's clubbers wanted to get high.

By the time they'd got home, Lorenzo's shoulders were aching with tension. He'd picked up a decent bottle of red and took it up to his room where Harry lay on the bed, dozing. He woke up when he heard the door go.

"Have you been in here all day?" Lorenzo asked.

"You told me to."

"Does that make you my sex slave?"

"If the position is vacant, I'd definitely apply."

Sitting down on the bed, Lorenzo stretched his arms above his head. The amount of clicking involved alarmed him. He was getting old.

Harry crawled up behind him and massaged his shoulders. His nimble fingers went straight to the source of the ache and the delicious release made Lorenzo cry out.

"Sssh." Harry laughed. "They'll think I've leapt on you as soon as you walked in the door."

"You're only human."

Harry continued kneading at Lorenzo's knots. "So much tension. How has your day been?"

"Brooks is pissed. We've got some stock, but nowhere near enough. The dealers are going berserk."

"Gary isn't the most reasonable of men. Surely he's not blaming you?"

Lorenzo dropped his head as Harry manipulated his spine. God this man had the touch of an angel. "Blame doesn't come into it. He says he won't lose the supply line into Manchester. If I don't get that stock, he's going to cut a deal with Wellingham."

"Fuck."

"Fuck indeed."

They sat in silence for a while. Harry continued working his way around Lorenzo's shoulders. It felt companionable, something Lorenzo hadn't experienced in such a long time.

When he'd finished, Harry patted Lorenzo on the shoulder. "For the next part of my de-stress treatment, you are eligible for a cuddle. Would you like to redeem that now?"

"Oh, I'd bloody love it."

Harry scooted back on the bed and held his arms out. Lorenzo allowed himself to be wrapped in them, resting his head on Harry's chest. His system became calm.

"Have you any idea what we're going to do?" Lorenzo asked. "It feels like things are getting out of control. If we don't act quickly, we're leaving ourselves wide open to that slimy piece of shit."

He could hear Harry's heartbeat. Lorenzo ran his hand over Harry's chest. Protecting that heart was becoming his sole focus in life.

"I think so," Harry said. "I need to work some things out."

"Mr Mystery." Lorenzo chuckled. "I like it. It's sexy."

"We have two choices," Harry continued. "Stealth or force. It's up to you."

Both had their attractions. "I don't care as long as Wellingham gets what he deserves."

"I meant what I said," Harry replied. "No shootings. I can't lose you twice."

"Fine." Lorenzo raised his head and scooted up Harry's body, so they were face-to-face. "I don't even own a gun. I leave that to others."

Before Harry could answer, he kissed him. When their lips met, it was always fire. He couldn't get enough of him. "Did you say something about being my sex slave?" Lorenzo asked. "I'm sure you did."

Harry spun Lorenzo and straddled him. "I did. As you hold the key to my safety, I should repay the favour by doing anything you say."

Just Harry saying the words made Lorenzo's cock spring to life. "Anything?"

Harry nodded.

"Take your clothes off. Slowly. Let me watch."

Obediently, Harry leapt off the bed. He stood at the foot and unbuttoned his shirt. Lorenzo palmed his groin. Harry took the shirt off and threw it on the chair.

Then he turned around. His firm, muscular arse filled his jeans perfectly.

Harry quickly undid the belt then slowly let his trousers drop to the floor. He had on skin-tight black boxer briefs. Lorenzo desperately wanted to rip them down and bury his face between Harry's butt cheeks. Yet he had named the game and he had to play by the rules.

Stepping out of his jeans and socks left Harry only in his underwear. He ran his hands over the cotton, outlining everything.

"Show me," Lorenzo murmured.

Inch by inch, Harry slid the boxers down, his dark, soft skin being revealed. Now fully naked, Harry leant on the dressing table, leaning forward so Lorenzo could indeed see everything.

The world of drugs and money and revenge seemed a million miles away. If Lorenzo could have locked that door forever, he would have done.

"Turn around," he instructed.

Harry did as he was told, his long dick standing proudly to attention.

"Can you really be mine?" Lorenzo said.

"All yours."

"Make me come," Lorenzo replied. "You choose how."

Slowly, Harry approached him, a glint in his eye. "Then that makes you mine."

Lorenzo ran his finger up Harry's muscular thigh. "We're each other's."

Roughly, Harry undid Lorenzo's button and fly. He reached inside and wrapped his fingers around Lorenzo's hard thick dick. The touch made Lorenzo cry out and he couldn't have cared less who heard it. "Make me come, baby," Lorenzo whispered.

Harry released Lorenzo's cock then ran the head through his fingers, stopping to wipe the pre-cum. He raised his thumb to his lips and tasted.

"Decisions, decisions," he said with a grin.

"You carry on teasing me like that and my dick might make the choice for you."

"I might have known you'd be no good at giving up control," Harry replied. "You've left me no choice."

He went to his open bag and found a tie. Gently he wrapped it around Lorenzo's wrist before tying it to the iron bedstead. With this unexpected turn of events, Lorenzo's balls were aching.

Next, Harry picked up his jeans and pulled the belt free. He attached Lorenzo's other hand to the bed. "Now the tables have turned."

He walked around the foot of the bed. Lorenzo took in every inch of his bulky frame. Harry reached into the drawers and retrieved a condom. Deftly, he unwrapped it and rolled it over Lorenzo's solid dick.

"Oh fuck," Lorenzo said.

Next, Harry applied lube to his hand. Once again he leant over the dressing table and ran his fingers over his hole. The gleaming lube made his skin shine as though it were made of gemstones.

Harry pushed one finger inside, then two. He stretched his own hole as Lorenzo could only watch, anticipation burning in every pore.

"Maybe I'll just sort myself out," Harry said, catching Lorenzo's eye in the mirror.

"Don't you dare," Lorenzo replied, straining against his ties.

Harry giggled. "As if I would settle for a wank when I have you in front of me."

He came over to the bed and in one motion straddled Lorenzo once more, running the tip of Lorenzo's cock down his arse.

"Kiss me," Lorenzo instructed.

Leaning forward, Harry stopped just as their breath mingled. He traced the outline of Lorenzo's mouth with his tongue. Then he leant back, reaching behind to steady Lorenzo's cock as he slowly eased it inside him. The warmth coming from Harry sparked joy inside Lorenzo. Painfully slowly, Harry slid down Lorenzo's shaft, his body enveloping him.

"Fuck," Harry said, exhaling slowly when he'd taken the full length of Lorenzo inside him.

"Ride me, baby," Lorenzo urged.

Slowly, Harry began to buck his hips. The contrast of Harry's naked body against Lorenzo's clothed one turned Lorenzo on all the more. Except for their connection, they were hardly touching.

"Faster," Lorenzo begged.

Harry shook his head. "All good things come to those who wait."

His pace was maddeningly slow. If he'd been free, Lorenzo would have bent him over the bed and fucked him hard. Instead, he'd given Harry control.

Playing with his own nipples, Harry stared at Lorenzo. "Fuck your dick feels good."

"Untie me," Lorenzo begged. "Please."

"Not a chance," Harry replied. "You have to learn to play by the rules, de Luca."

He rode him slightly faster now, but still nowhere near what Lorenzo craved. The show Harry put on while he did this was incredible. He roved his hands over his own body, rubbing and teasing himself while Lorenzo desperately wanted to feel his skin.

"If I let you go, what will happen?" Harry teased, maintaining the pace.

"You fucking know," Lorenzo replied.

"Tell me."

"I'll fuck you into tomorrow."

"Is that a promise?"

"Too right it is. Do it."

Harry got up off the bed. Instantly, Lorenzo missed the warm comfort of Harry's body.

"Very well. We did say your wish is my command."

He gently undid the tie. Lorenzo scrambled to get his hand free then reached over and undid the belt. By the time he looked up, Harry had bent over the dressing table. Lorenzo couldn't wait anymore. He bolted off the bed and pushed his cock deep inside Harry who cried out.

"Fuck me, Lorenzo. Hard."

With his pants around his ankles, Lorenzo gripped onto Harry's hips and pounded his hole for all he was worth.

"Come for me," Lorenzo ordered. "Now."

Harry reached underneath his body and started to tug at his dick. Lorenzo was close and he wanted it all tonight.

"Don't stop, Lorenzo," Harry panted. "I'm coming."

He leant forward, his body tensing—his orgasm contracting all his muscles. This was the final straw for Lorenzo, who let out a moan. The flash of sweet detachment overwhelmed him as the release gripped every part of his body. Digging his nails into Harry's soft skin, he filled the condom. His eyes were seeing stars when he opened them. Still inside Harry, he leant forward and kissed his sweaty back.

"You are fucking incredible," he whispered.

"And all yours," Harry replied. "Forever."

Chapter Seventeen

They walked over the brow of the hill. The perimeter fence that the lads had put up when they first arrived stood eight feet high, was razor-sharp at the top and alarmed to within an inch of its life. No one was getting in.

Harry stared up at the construction. "You mean business."

"Too right I do. Look at what happened when Marco took his eye off the ball."

Harry couldn't meet Lorenzo's gaze. "I'm not going to lie and say I didn't help plan that, Lorenzo. Of course I did."

"Harry, we've both done terrible things in our time. Sometimes we were on the same side and others we weren't."

Now Harry did meet his stare. "If I'd known it was you, I wouldn't have done it."

"Pah," Lorenzo said, waving him away. "Of course, you would. Jonny Wellingham has a way of persuading people. No one in that farm blames you. I need you to prove your worth to them. They won't keep protecting you just because I'm fucking you."

Harry raised an eyebrow. "They might think I'm fucking you."

"Trust me," Lorenzo said, playfully shoving him on the shoulder. "They know who the top is."

"Big man." Harry laughed. "One day, I'll show you how strong you have to be to take eight inches. Then we'll see who has the power."

They carried on walking. The view was spectacular. Manchester's skyline shimmered in the distance, dominated by the tower in which Lorenzo had his only remaining product that wouldn't satisfy Greg Brooks totally.

"I mean what I say," Lorenzo said. "You need to help us."

Harry had a fierce determination on his face. "How about we get the majority of your stock as well as fixing Jonny Wellingham once and for all?"

This is a turn up for the books. "I'm listening."

"The one thing Jonny fears more than even death is what?"

Lorenzo thought for a second. "Prison."

"Exactly. If we were to get him in the same location as a fraction of what he stole from you, he would be going down for a very long time."

"How would we do it?"

"That's where my plan comes in. First we have to know where the stuff is. Now I've got a fair idea. Jonny has drops all over the city. Not many are big enough to hold that much. My guess is he's got it in a garage in Trafford Park."

It made sense that Jonny wouldn't split the stuff. He had no way to offload it yet. The dealers were still sticking with Greg Brooks. If Lorenzo could get at least two crates and leave one for Jonny, they would have more than enough for the foreseeable future.

"I like it. What's your plan for getting it out?"

"Easy," Harry said, as they set off down the hill. "If we let Jonny know we're planning a raid, he'll panic and want to move it. I know that man — he wants it all."

"Remind you of someone?"

"Just a bit," Harry agreed. "He'll leave enough there to tempt you into the open. The rest will go in a van somewhere. Probably his old gaff. He's not been there since the fire. Even so, he had the gate fixed. It's still like Fort Knox."

The idea sent tingles up Lorenzo's spine. This had been his dream when he'd begged Harry to join him. Over the years, Lorenzo had learnt strategy. Harry had always been naturally gifted. It made Lorenzo's mouth water that Harry was turning it on Jonny.

"There's only one problem," Lorenzo said.

"What's that?"

"We don't know for definite it's in the garage."

* * * *

The ground was cold and stank of rotting food. Lorenzo turned his nose up but refused to show weakness.

"Can you see anything?" he asked Harry, who had binoculars trained on a garage.

"There's a van," Harry replied. "Plus, there's three lads on guard duty. Not normal for a garage."

Lorenzo needed more than that. He wasn't about to send his people into danger on a hunch, no matter how attractive the person it came from was. "They can't be hiding three crates that easily," Lorenzo grumbled. "Can't we get closer?"

They were hiding in a council refuse site. Every now and again, a worker would come too close, meaning they had to crouch even lower. Lorenzo couldn't bear to think what filth he would be breathing in. When he got to the farm, a long hot shower was required. Hopefully, Harry could be persuaded to wash his back.

"If we scramble along the sides of those skips, I reckon we'll get a better view," Harry replied. He didn't wait for Lorenzo's reply before setting off.

Lorenzo followed him. They were close enough to the garage now that they could hear voices. Unfortunately, Lorenzo couldn't make out what was being said. Harry had got it right. They could see right through the double doors into the back of the building.

"What did you say you labelled them?" Harry asked.

"Ponti Pizza Bases. Marco's idea."

"Bingo," Harry said, handing him the binoculars.

Lorenzo trained them on the building. Sure enough three crates with about twelve boxes each sat there, each box emblazoned with the fake company. "Slimy thieving bastard," Lorenzo muttered.

"We should get out of here," Harry replied.

They retraced their steps and dashed through the refuse site to the car they'd parked on the other side. When they both got in, Lorenzo screwed his nose up. "Jesus, this car will be ruined."

"Baby, we'll be headed to Tuscany in a few days. Who cares?"

Lorenzo grinned at Harry. "When you put it like that, you're making my balls tingle."

"Ha, well, don't get any ideas. Not until you've washed them."

They drove out of the massive industrial estate. Trafford Park housed some of the country's biggest factories, making everything from breakfast cereal to detergents. It was the perfect cover.

"You're sure your copper mate isn't going to pull a fast one?"

Harry shook his head. "They've been after him for years. Ryan told me if I ever saw the light, he'd look after me. I'm afraid I probably won't be able to come to England again."

Lorenzo stared at the grey sky, the grey buildings and the grey faces of the people trudging along the pavements in the rain. "No worries on that score."

They chatted happily on the way home. Lorenzo marvelled at just how right things were with Harry by his side. For the thousandth time he regretted not getting word to him years ago. Truthfully, he hadn't fully trusted that Harry would come to him. Now as he listened to Harry's story about a holiday he'd taken in Barcelona, he wondered why on earth he hadn't had faith in their love.

Once they got to the farm, darkness had fallen. As they walked into the house, Lorenzo heard raised voices coming from the lounge. "What bloody now?" he exclaimed.

One of the lads came bursting out of the lounge, and Lorenzo grabbed him by the arm. "What's happening?"

"Marco and Gab, boss."

"What about them?"

"They had a fall-out."

He glared pointedly at Harry. Lorenzo could just guess what it was about. "Fine. On you go."

The lad scurried away, leaving Lorenzo to take a deep breath. Just as he braced himself to go into battle, Harry placed a hand on his shoulder. "Can I?"

"You sure?"

"Yeah, just be there to back me up."

Lorenzo shrugged. If Harry wanted to handle it, who was he to stand in his way. "On you go then."

Harry walked into the lounge, closely followed by Lorenzo. Gabriel and Marco were nose to nose. Liam was trying to shove Marco away, and Fed sat on the sofa, watching. A few of the lads were dotted around the room.

"How do you know he's not spying for Wellingham right now?" Marco snarled.

"And what would I tell him?" Harry said.

Everyone snapped to attention. Marco had the decency to look shamefaced "I'm sorry, Harry. It's true—ever since you got here, we've been treading water while Wellingham finds an outlet for our product. It wouldn't surprise me if you vanish in a puff of smoke any day."

Lorenzo's first instinct was to slap his nephew around the head. Then he took a second and realised it was a fair theory. Of course, it was bullshit, but seeing things from Marco's point of view, they were very different.

Harry stared at each figure in the room. "You're all right to be wary. Lorenzo and I have a plan. Liam, Marco, can we speak with you?"

They joined Lorenzo at the door.

"Oh, and by the way," Harry said, "I stink of shit, and I think I have at least three used tea bags about my person. God knows what else. Just in case you were doubting my commitment."

Gabriel wafted his hand in front of his nose. "You do stink a bit."

"All in a day's work, Gabriel," Harry said.

Always a believer in quitting while he was ahead, Lorenzo shoved Marco out of the room. "You need to calm the fuck down," he whispered. "I won't tell you again about Harry."

* * * *

"Run that past me again," Marco blurted out. "Your plan is to grass Jonny up to the coppers?"

"Don't be so childish, Marco," Lorenzo snarled. "This isn't the movies. This is real life, and it gets dirty. We fight with every weapon we have."

They were crammed in the little office room, Lorenzo fighting the urge to give his nephew a slap. His behaviour in the last ten minutes had been absolutely unacceptable.

"He's right," Liam said. "Jonny used to shit himself if he thought the law were watching. So how we going to get him there?"

Harry had been watching nervously until that moment, and now he walked over to the window. "We trip the alarm. There's a couple of guards on and if we go at night, the garage staff will be long gone."

"It has to be us four only. Possibly Gab and Fed. There could be another leak. I wouldn't put it past Tommasso to turn one of the lads."

Marco nodded. "Yeah, good call. Right, Uncle, I will do this because I love you. Harry, every time I run my tongue over the gap in my teeth, I want to smash your face in. I will respect my uncle's wishes. This is your chance to change my mind."

"Just a minute," Lorenzo barked.

"It's okay, Lorenzo," Harry said. "I appreciate your honesty, Marco. I hope I can do that."

"I'll tell Tommasso," Liam said. "He'll suspect me less of feeding him a load of shite."

Lorenzo laughed. "I don't know what you're saying about me and my nephew here, Liam. I will agree regardless."

Liam reddened, which made Lorenzo giggle all the more.

"We could do with getting people moving out there. They're all in the lounge," Marco said.

"Leave that to me." Lorenzo grinned.

He led them out of the office and into the lounge. It was crammed with people all watching a football match now the floor show provided by Marco and Gab had finished. Gab glanced at him nervously. Lorenzo simply nodded his head and winked. He wouldn't forget the loyalty Gab had shown him.

"Okay, boys." Lorenzo clapped his hands. "It's takeaway night. You have precisely ten minutes to get your orders in before Tommasso here goes to the Chinese."

The lads all cheered.

"Why me, boss?" Tommasso whined.

"Because you love to drive," Lorenzo replied. "And nothing pleases you more than doing something for your fellow man."

For a second, he worried he had gone too far. He had completely failed to keep the venom out of his voice. Thankfully it went right over Tommasso's head.

"Fine." He sighed.

"What are you waiting for?" Lorenzo said to the room.

They all leapt up and dashed to the kitchen where the menus were. Lorenzo intercepted Gab and Fed in the hallway. "Office, please."

They followed him in, both shifting nervously in front of him. His heart went out to them. Having to watch the net curl around Tommasso must be excruciating for them.

"I'm sorry to have to ask this of you. Liam is telling Tommasso something now that he will want to tell this girl as soon as. I want you to follow him and find out who she is. Chances are he'll just call her. If he's cock blind over her, they might meet up. We could get lucky."

Gab nodded, but Fed looked uncomfortable. "This is really hard, boss. Isn't there anyone else who could do it?"

Lorenzo shook his head. "I know I'm asking a lot of you, Fed. Believe me. None of the lads aren't experienced enough for this. I can only trust you two. Marco and Liam are working on something with me."

Gab glanced at Fed. "We understand that you want to keep it between yourselves. We want you to know we're here if you need us."

Lorenzo squeezed his knee. "That's more help that you know. For now, we need to neutralise Tommasso until I decide what to do with him. When he gets home, he's under house arrest. The lads don't need to know any more than he's not allowed out of his room."

Fed nodded. "I thought something similar. Thank you, boss. For being so...flexible."

"I said this to Marco earlier. We are not living in a movie. We do what we please and Tommasso is family.

Mark my words, I'll think up a suitable punishment for him so that no one will see betraying Lorenzo de Luca as a good idea. Now scram or you'll miss out on your food."

They grinned and opened the door. Lorenzo's heart leapt when he saw Harry leaning against the wall. Fed and Gab nodded to Harry before heading off to the kitchen. Lorenzo held his arms out. "Come to me," he said.

Harry strolled into the office, closing the door behind him. Lorenzo pulled him onto his knee and nuzzled his chest. "What a fucking day."

"You're incredible," Harry said, kissing the top of his head. "I always knew you would be a good leader, back in the day. Seeing the way you treat your lads and the respect they have for you…I'm so proud of you."

Tears glistened in Lorenzo's eyes. He was good at what he did. The success of the family stood testament to that. Hearing the words come from Harry mainlined straight to his heart. "Thank you," he said, meekly. "You spoke well too."

Harry squeezed him. "I had to. Their respect will be hard earned, Lorenzo, and that's as it should be. I'll do it, though."

"You might not get the chance."

"What?"

"Because we might be in Tuscany instead where the only worry will be whether to have white or red with dinner."

"Can you really do it?" Harry asked, stroking his ear.

"Leave it all?" Lorenzo replied. "With your hand in mine, I can do anything."

Harry reached down and took hold of Lorenzo's hand. They sat there for a while, listening to the hubbub outside and enjoying the stillness.

The calm before the storm.

Chapter Eighteen

Tommasso took over an hour to come back with the food. The lads were chomping at the bit. That was nothing compared to Lorenzo. Harry had gone upstairs to speak to his copper friend and Lorenzo thought it best if he did that alone.

"Have you called them?" he asked Marco.

"Since the last time?"

"Come with me."

Lorenzo led Marco out of the busy lounge and into the farmyard. The biting cold made them scurry across the tarmac and to one of the SUVs parked up.

"Fuck me, it's freezing," Marco complained, as they hopped in. "It's nights like this I miss home."

"I need to talk to you. Away from everyone else," Lorenzo said, his teeth chattering. Why hadn't he brought a key so he could put the heater on?

"Okay," Marco said uncertainly. "Why does that fill me with dread?"

Lorenzo chuckled and stared at his nephew fondly. "Because you have trust issues. You're growing into a wise young man."

"Go on then," Marco replied. "What's on your mind?"

The plan had been set, although something hadn't felt right to Lorenzo. "I can't argue that Jonny fears prison—he's shit scared of it. He'll get the best lawyers in the land. They'll get him off on a piss-weak sentence. In no time he'll be out to cause us trouble again."

Marco frowned. "What are you saying?"

"As soon as we've sorted Jonny," Lorenzo began, "Harry and I are getting out of here. I'm done with it all, little one. I've messaged Enzo and asked him to get the villa ready."

Marco raised an eyebrow. "That soon?"

Lorenzo nodded. "This business with Tommasso has made me realise it's time for me to give way. Harry and I could never run Manchester. Too much has gone on. The dealers wouldn't trust it. The city needs stability."

If poor Marco tried to keep the hope from his face, he failed spectacularly. His burning ambition made Lorenzo's heart swell. He saw so much of himself in the boy. "I have an offer to make you," he said.

"Oh, yes?" Marco replied.

"You'll have control on one condition."

Marco frowned. "What's that?"

"Only while you remain with Liam," Lorenzo announced. "I mean it, Marco. You're too much of a loose cannon with him. If, for whatever reason, your relationship fails, I'll send someone to take over."

He could see this condition rankled with Marco, who sensibly kept his thoughts to himself.

"It won't be a problem," Marco said. "Because Liam and I are together, no matter what happens. I love him, Uncle. More than anything."

Lorenzo nodded. "That's good. He's been the making of you, little one."

"What's all the rush?" Marco asked. "You're making it sound like an escape plan instead of retirement. I thought Harry's plan meant no one had to do that."

Lorenzo rubbed the bridge of his nose. What had started as his life's work now obstructed everything. He'd be glad when it was all over and they might find some peace. "Just between you and me, I have a more permanent solution to the Wellingham problem."

Marco's eyes widened. "You're going to kill him?"

"Not a word of this," Lorenzo replied. "I mean it, Marco. I'll go along with Harry's plan until we get Jonny in the open. Then I'm going to put three bullets in him like he did to me. Although I won't be fucking stupid enough to fail."

Shaking his head, Marco looked uneasy. "What will Harry say?"

"Do you even care?"

"I care about you, and you care about him. So, I suppose I do in a third-hand sort of way."

If that constituted a thaw, it was minuscule, but Lorenzo would take it. "He'll forgive me once we get to Italy. We can frame one of his stupid kid army and the police will be satisfied. Let's face it, they aren't going to investigate too much. They just want him gone."

Before Marco could reply, headlights lit up the place.

"Tommasso is here," Lorenzo said.

Sure enough, as they got out of the car, Tommasso parked up next to them.

"Hey, boss," he said, hopping out. "What are you two up to? Having a secret meeting?"

"Got it in one," Lorenzo said. "Take the food in and come back out straight away. I need to talk to you about something. We'll be in the barn."

Tommasso glanced nervously at them. "Okay, what's up?"

"No need to look like you've shit yourself," Marco said with a chuckle. "It's about the safe hatch. We were thinking we probably need a few more now we've grown. I said you'd be the best at heading it up."

Tommasso grinned. "Dead right I am. Give me five minutes."

He scurried off towards the house. Lorenzo's heart was breaking at this treachery. He had done more bad things than he cared to admit, but selling out the family? *Never.*

"Good thinking, little one," Lorenzo said. "Fuck, this is killing me."

Clapping him on the shoulder, Marco led him into the barn. Weightlifting equipment littered it. When the cold snap had come, not many people had had the desire to bother exercising out here.

"When Enzo found us in there and realised who was missing," Marco said, quietly, "I'll never forget the look on his face."

Rage swelled inside Lorenzo. "That's why Jonny fucking Wellingham deserves more than a cushy prison cell. The scumbag deserves to know what real fear is."

Lights flooded the place again and another SUV pulled up in the yard. Fed and Gab got out.

"We're in here," Marco called.

They dashed in, both lads as white as sheets.

"Well?" Lorenzo asked.

"You're not going to believe it," Fed began. "It's Sadie Wellingham. He met her at a fucking layby. She was all over him like herpes."

Lorenzo sank down on one of the weight benches and put his head in his hands. He'd expected it to be one of the few working girls still loyal to Jonny. He could almost admire Tommasso for going straight to the top.

"Fuck, Wellingham must be desperate if he's sending his princess into battle," Marco said. "I don't think much of Tommasso's taste. She's a rotten little bitch. Liam's told me all about her."

The light from the house streamed out as the door opened. "He's coming," Lorenzo said, getting back up. He smoothed his jacket and tried to get his head together.

They all stood up straight. Each one of them looked nervous. Lorenzo had never expected to find himself in this position.

"What's going on here?" Tommasso said. "A mothers' meeting?"

Lorenzo nodded at Gab and Fed, who moved forward. Before Tommasso realised he was in trouble, they had him by the tops of the arms and Fed and Gab dragged him over to one of the weight benches and slammed him down.

"What the fuck are you doing?" Tommasso blustered. "Stop fucking about. Our dinner'll be getting cold."

Tommasso struggled but it was pointless. Lorenzo bent forward. "Sadie Wellingham?"

The colour drained from Tommasso's face. "What about her?"

"Let's not play that game," Lorenzo continued. "Fed and Gab followed you tonight. You couldn't wait to report that story Liam told you."

Tommasso's eyes widened. "Boss, I can explain. "

"So can I. You got caught up in that fucking fire-damaged honeytrap and sold your family out for a bit of skirt."

His life might have been hanging in the balance, but Tommasso had the courage to scowl. "I learnt from the best, didn't I?"

Lorenzo slapped him across the head. "Don't you dare try to deflect onto me, you little fuck. I never put anyone's life in danger, and neither did Marco. But you. You've been telling them God knows what. Is she really that good at sucking cock?"

"It's not like that," Tommasso muttered. "We're properly together. We love each other."

The ridiculousness of it all broke Lorenzo's heart. "Don't be so stupid. She doesn't give a fuck about you. I bet she won't even try to get in touch when you go quiet."

Fear marched across Tommasso's face. "When I go quiet?"

"Yes. You're out of action, Tommasso. You'll be held in one of the campervans until tonight, then you'll be flying to Italy with Harry and me. Think yourself fucking lucky you're not in an unmarked grave somewhere."

Tommasso struggled. "You can't just kidnap me."

Lorenzo stared into his nephew's eyes. "You can leave at any time. Believe me, you wouldn't make it to daybreak when Wellingham finds out you've just led him into a trap. Your choice."

* * * *

After they had secured Tommasso and Gab had taken the first shift, Lorenzo went upstairs. Harry sat on the bed, staring into space.

"What are you doing in the dark?" Lorenzo asked.

"Thinking."

Lorenzo turned the light on and to his dismay a gun sat on his pillow next to where Harry sat. "Now wait…"

"I'm thinking about how everyone is a fucking liar. You, Jonny and me. We've lied for so long we don't know how to tell the truth anymore."

Lorenzo moved closer to the bed. Harry shifted his legs out of reach. "Don't touch me."

"Harry, please. You're spinning."

"Of course I am," Harry replied. "You told me you didn't have a gun. I decided to put some of my things away and what do I find? This? It's not made of chocolate, so I presume it's a fully working gun."

Lorenzo sat on the end of the bed. "I forgot I even had it. When we first got here, everyone had one. Your boss had killed two people, if you remember. I wasn't sure he wouldn't try it again. Let's face it, imagination has never been Jonny's strongest suit."

"That's where I came in most of the time," Harry muttered.

Tentatively, Lorenzo reached for his ankle. Was it a good sign that he didn't pull away again? Lorenzo stroked the skin at the top of Harry's sock. It was the only thing he could think of doing to calm him.

This might be one of the last nights they would spend in the room. It had become stifling and claustrophobic. Once they got to the villa with the sunshine and beautiful gardens, things would be so much better. He couldn't wait to wake up every morning with Harry. They could explore the countryside and find all the best places to eat. It was days away.

"Am I forgiven?" Lorenzo ventured.

"Fuck, I don't know which way is up anymore." Harry scrubbed his face with his hands. "If this is going to work, you have to share everything with me, Lorenzo. If we can't trust each other, we might as well call it a day."

"I told you, I'd forgotten I even had it. Honestly."

Harry frowned. "You must have a lot of firepower here if you can just casually forget a gun."

Lorenzo hated being questioned, even by Harry. Ever since Papa had died, he had made all the decisions on his own. Being part of a team again would take some getting used to.

"You're safe because of that," he muttered. "I didn't hear you complaining when Jonny was after your arse. I suppose you only had water pistols when you were with him."

The tension in the room could have been cut with a knife.

"I know you hate him," Harry continued. "I don't blame you. Nobody would. You told me that Marco needs to learn strategy. What example would you be setting him if you blow Jonny's brains out?"

"Okay, fine. I intended to take it with me as protection," Lorenzo admitted. "They'll be armed. Jonny could go crazy if he thinks he's cornered. You'll be his first target, then me."

"I wonder how much of an excuse you'd need? Jesus Christ, Lorenzo. Let the others be armed. It isn't as personal for them. Please."

Lorenzo loved how much Harry cared for their future. He wished Marco could see the urgency on Harry's face right now. How protective he was over Lorenzo.

"Fine," Lorenzo said. "Tomorrow, I'll hand it over to Marco like a good boy. Is that good enough for you?"

To his relief, Harry held his arms out for him. Lorenzo crawled up the bed and snuggled into him. "I don't like fighting with you."

"Me neither. I can't lose you, Lorenzo. Not to him."

"You won't."

They lay in silence for a while.

"Tommasso has been fucking Sadie," Lorenzo announced.

Harry tensed. "Are you sure?"

"Got it from his lips. He thinks they're in love."

Harry exhaled loudly. "Shit, Jonny has made some unusual moves lately."

"That's because you're not around."

"I guess."

"I love you."

Sighing, Harry squeezed him close. "I love you too. We should get some sleep. I spoke to my contact at the police. They want us to make the move in a couple of days."

It was happening quickly, but that suited Lorenzo. The whole thing hung over them like a raincloud. "Fine, I'll let Marco and Liam know tomorrow."

"We should get some sleep," Harry replied. "God knows what tomorrow will bring."

Chapter Nineteen

Lorenzo sat bolt upright in bed, his heart racing. He could swear he'd heard a bang. Instinctively reaching for Harry to wake him, he found his side of the bed empty.

He must have gone to the toilet. Lorenzo rubbed his eyes. He couldn't shake the unease in his system. The house lay absolutely still. Glancing at his watch showed him it had just gone two a.m.

Then he heard a car door shut.

Fear gripped his body as he scrambled out of bed and to the window. The yard was empty, so perhaps he'd imagined it. Then suddenly one of the SUVs burst into life. The lights lit up the occupant and at that moment Lorenzo's stomach left him.

It was Harry.

What the fuck was he doing? Before Lorenzo could get the window open to shout to him, he had sped out of the yard.

Stark naked, Lorenzo glanced around the room. On the dressing table sat a small piece of paper bearing the words *I can't trust you.*

"Fuck," Lorenzo shouted.

He quickly threw on his jeans and shirt. Stealing out onto the landing, there wasn't any movement, although the lads on guard duty wouldn't have missed Harry's getaway.

Lorenzo dashed into Marco and Liam's room. They were fast asleep in each other's arms. At any other time, it would have been a lovely scene. Lorenzo had no time for sentiment. "Wake up, both of you," he whispered, roughly shaking Marco.

They both stirred then sprang to life immediately at seeing Lorenzo standing over them.

"Uncle, what is it?" Marco sat.

"Harry. He's taken one of the SUVs and fucked off."

Liam flicked the lamp on, illuminating the room in a warm, golden glow. "What?" he asked. "What happened?"

"I don't know. You have to get up. We need to follow him."

Marco rubbed his eyes. "You don't even know where he's headed. He could be going anywhere. I fucking knew this would happen. What did I say?"

Liam shoved him. "Marco, shut up. Lorenzo, do you have any idea what the fuck is going on?"

"I do," Lorenzo said. "He's gone to the garage."

"Why?" Liam asked, fully awake now. "We're not hitting it for days."

Lorenzo sunk onto the bed. "He found my gun. I was sure I'd convinced him I had it just for protection. I don't think he believed me."

"Clearly not." Marco groaned, sinking onto the pillow.

"Come on," Lorenzo said. "If I know Harry, he's gone to trigger the alarms."

"He won't stand a chance on his own," Liam cut in.

"That's why I need you to fucking move."

"Could you give us some privacy then?" Marco grumbled.

"For fuck's sake, I wiped that arse enough times. Fine, you have five minutes. Move it, the pair of you."

Lorenzo ran across the landing and into Claire's room. She yelped when he came in. "What the fuck are you doing? I heard you wake those two up."

"Claire, listen," Lorenzo whispered. "Harry has fucked off. He's gone to trigger the alarms."

Claire hugged her knees to her. "Already? On his own? What the fuck's going on?"

To his relief he heard Liam and Marco heading down the stairs. "I haven't got time to go into it. Do me a favour. Book three seats on the first flight out of here. Anywhere on the mainland of Italy we can hire a car. The shit might hit the fan."

"Three?"

"Me, Harry and Tommasso. That little shit doesn't leave my sight. Once you've done that, speak to Gab and Fed. I want them ready to move."

Claire nodded. "Good luck, Lorenzo. Finish that cunt off good and proper."

He kissed her cheek. "One way or the other, Jonny Wellingham won't be a problem after tonight. Of that I can promise you."

* * * *

They parked in exactly the place where he and Harry had parked previously. Things were happening at a breakneck speed. It felt like a lifetime ago that they'd negotiated stinking rubbish for the greater good.

Liam and Marco stared at him in fear.

"What do we do now, Uncle?" Marco whispered.

"I'll go closer and see what the fuck is going on," Lorenzo replied. He checked his pocket. The gun was there. He would shoot every single person before he let them touch Harry. "You ring the police again. They should be here by now if Harry has called them."

"I'm not ringing the fucking police," Marco replied.

"Jesus Christ, I'll do it," Liam said, glaring at Marco.

"Good lad," Lorenzo said. "Keep the engine running. We will need to get out of here quickly, no matter what happens. Liam, you drive. Marco, get ready to cover us."

Marco nodded grimly.

Lorenzo tried to focus. He could pull this off, no matter what Harry thought. They were having a future together if he had to move heaven and earth.

"I love you, Uncle," Marco said, as Lorenzo opened the door.

Lorenzo kissed his nephew's hand. "I love you too, little one."

He scrambled out of the car and into the cold night air. His breath smoke in front of him as he made his way around the perimeter fencing of the refuse centre. With the night protecting him, he didn't need to crawl through mounds of crap this time.

When he got within sight of the garage, his heart dropped. About ten lads were dotted around and in the centre knelt Harry with his hands behind his head. Floodlights lit up the forecourt and there stood Jonny Wellingham with a gun to Harry's forehead.

Lorenzo's first instinct was to kill Jonny. Where he crouched, he couldn't be sure of a clean shot. He needed to get closer.

As stealthily as possible while his heart hammered away in his chest, Lorenzo skirted around the building. They had parked close enough for him to use their cars as cover.

Sloppy, Jonny. Very sloppy indeed.

Peering over the bonnet, he could just make out what they were saying. The gang were all here – even Deano stood near to Jonny. He was still supporting himself on a crutch. It gladdened Lorenzo's heart that when the police did show up, he wouldn't stand a chance even if the rest got away.

"He's not showing, boss," Deano said. "Let's just finish that piece of shit. It'll be just as good letting him come and find his bum buddy's body."

Jonny shook his head. "He'll show. As soon as he realises his bed is cold, he'll know where this lying little prick has gone."

Deano sighed. The bloodthirsty fuck couldn't wait. Lorenzo wondered how well he would fare in prison without Jonny to protect him.

Lorenzo's phone vibrated in his pocket. He dove down behind the car and eased it out. He had the screen on night mode. He could still make out a message from Liam. They were on their way.

All he had to do now was get Harry out of there.

"Move the gear," Jonny said to two of the lads. "Take the vans to the house. I'm not losing it all. Just enough to tempt Lorenzo out of his hole. Brooks will be begging me tomorrow when he finds out his little mates are in the ship canal."

Jonny Wellingham remained depressingly easy to predict. Even if everything went tits up that night,

Jonny was finished. Without Harry to advise him, he was just a brainless thug with no remorse. Even if he and Harry died that night, Marco would do the rest. Of that, Lorenzo had no fear.

He peered over the bonnet again. Jonny stood in front of Harry. "I'm not going to lie, Harry," Jonny said. "I didn't see this coming. You've hurt me. After everything we've been through, you can turn on me like this."

"You killed the only person I've ever loved," Harry replied. "Or at least I thought you had."

Jonny ran his hand over Harry's head. "Oh, Harry, and there I was thinking you only had eyes for me. You certainly fooled us all. I'll give you that. It will pain me to put a bullet between your eyes."

Harry laughed. "We both know you won't do that. You'll get one of these dumb bastards to do it. Jonny's scared of the clink, lads, did you know that? He'll hide behind you every time."

A couple of the lads shifted uncomfortably. Rage filled Jonny's face and he slapped Harry hard. "Don't worry, Harry. I'll make an exception for your deceitful fucking arse."

Lorenzo doubted that very much. Then again, if Jonny would resort to using his precious daughter as a honeytrap, he had to be desperate. Not a good sign right now.

"Go on then," Harry goaded him. "Show the lads what a big man you are."

Jonny clicked the safety off. Lorenzo couldn't stand and watch. He had to do something. He saw Harry close his eyes, ready to accept whatever the future had in store for him.

Lorenzo hadn't been a great believer in fate. He preferred to control his own destiny. So, he stood.

Deano was the first person to see him. "Boss," he shouted.

Harry flinched at the sound. Jonny spun around and when he locked eyes with Lorenzo, he grinned cruelly. "And who do we have here?" he said. "Harry's new owner has come. What's the matter, Lorenzo? Your dick get cold?"

Two of the lads tried to move over to the car where Lorenzo stood. He held his hand out. "Don't even try it, you stupid little fuckers."

"Leave him," Jonny roared. "Come closer, Lorenzo."

Lorenzo swaggered towards the centre of the circle. He wanted to dash to Harry and wrap his arms around him, but there was a game to be played and only one winner would emerge.

Instead, he wandered over maddeningly slowly. Maintaining eye contact with every scowling face that watched him, he allowed cocky Lorenzo to take over. When he reached Jonny, he grimaced. "Not getting any prettier, Jon. Unlike your slag of a daughter. Even with the obvious scarring, she's not bad. Tommasso said she's quite the goer."

Jonny went to strike Lorenzo then stopped as Lorenzo trained the gun on him. "You didn't even have me searched. It's not just your arse that's sagging. You've lost it, Wellingham. Everyone knows it."

"It probably makes you feel better to think it. Greg Brooks is interested in this consignment," Jonny lied. "If you had any delusions about robbing it, you're too late. Go for it, lads."

Two vans burst into life. They were driven by frightened kids who should be at home, tucked up in bed. Some of the other lads got out of the way as the vans drove across the forecourt and onto the road.

"Wave goodbye to your stock, de Luca," Jonny cackled. "You put up a good fight, it's true. Taking Harry from me was pretty unexpected. No one is indispensable. My darling Sadie is showing a lot of promise. Maybe I'll promote her."

Lorenzo grinned. "She'll need something to take her mind off things, now she isn't fucking my nephew."

"He can go where he likes," Jonny said. "You don't own him."

"I can guarantee, you won't be seeing him again."

Jonny glanced at Deano. "Well, well, well, Deano. Have you heard this? De Luca has wasted his own nephew."

"Fucking scum," Deano spat.

Lorenzo couldn't bring himself to look at Harry. The mask would slip as soon as he stared into those deep eyes.

"A shame too," Jonny continued. "When you two are dead, your little pink army will retreat. Tell you what, for old time's sake, I'll let them. How does that sound? All fuck off back to pastaland where you belong."

"Very gracious of you, Jon."

Just as Jonny was about to form another snarky reply, the sky lit up with blue and the ear-piercing sound of sirens reverberated around the buildings.

"What the fuck have you done?" Jonny screamed.

All hell broke loose as police cars and vans tore around the corner. Some of the lads panicked and one let off a shot. It glanced off the bonnet of a police car, but the ante had been upped now. As police gunmen spilled out of the vans and Wellingham's Boys took cover, Lorenzo grabbed Harry by the collar of his shirt and hauled him to his feet.

"We run," Lorenzo urged.

Mercifully, the way Lorenzo had come was clear. As they dashed across, Deano appeared from behind the car, a baseball bat in his hands.

"Where the fuck are you two going?"

Harry kicked him hard in the knee. Deano let out an almighty wail. "Fuck off, Deano," Harry spat at him.

They set off over the ridge. Once they got there, Lorenzo breathed a sigh of relief. In the shadows they were safer.

"The helicopter will be here at any minute," Harry said. "Let's just get the fuck out of here."

"Follow me."

Crouching down, they ran along the perimeter fence and to where Lorenzo had left Liam and Marco. The only problem was, they weren't there.

Fear gripped Lorenzo. Had they been picked up? They might have shopped Wellingham to the police, but they had to leave no trace. If they were caught red-handed, no plea deal would keep them out of prison. "Shit," Lorenzo said, pushing Harry against the fence. "Wait one second."

He got his mobile out and rang Marco.

"Uncle?"

"Where the fuck are you?"

"We had to move. The cops were getting way too close. The factory on the other side of the train tracks. Perseus Soap. We're in the car park."

"Well done." Lorenzo terminated the call.

On their reconnaissance mission, Harry had identified the factory car park as a potential fall-back point. He reasoned that people on foot were harder to trace heading over train tracks and through undergrowth than running along pavements.

They dashed towards the ramshackle fencing that was supposed to keep the public away. It was easy to clamber over and run down the banking. Lorenzo tore ahead, cursing the moonlight that gave his position away when he ran across the tracks.

On the other side, he searched frantically until he found a bit with a gap in the bottom. It would be a squeeze, but they could do it.

"You go first, quickly," he said.

He never heard anything in reply.

"Harry —"

He turned and almost lost his footing. Jonny Wellingham had his arm around Harry's neck and a gun to his temple.

Chapter Twenty

He still had the gun he'd trained on Wellingham, but Lorenzo wouldn't risk blowing Harry's head off in the process of killing Jonny. Fear was in Harry's eyes as he stared wildly towards Lorenzo.

"I'll take you both down with me." Jonny sneered.

"You'll only get one, old man," Lorenzo replied. "Unless my nephew gets you first. He'll have you in his sights right now."

Jonny laughed. "Where is he? In that tree? That was weak, Lorenzo."

It had been worth a try. Fed was miles away at the farm, keeping an eye on another headache of Lorenzo's.

Harry struggled and Jonny pressed the gun harder into his temple, making him cry out. Lorenzo took a step forward.

"I'll do it," Jonny shouted. "I don't give a fuck anymore."

Suddenly, the unmistakable sound of a helicopter approaching filled the air. Panic swept across Jonny's face.

"We need to get out of here," Jonny said. "Or we're all fucked. Don't be a dick, Lorenzo."

Grinning, Lorenzo took another step forward. "We're clean, Jon. Harry and I were simply out for a romantic stroll. Then you leap out of the bushes and take one of us hostage. It's self-defence really. I don't think they'll take kindly to your boys shooting at them either. I wonder if any cops have been killed yet. They hate that."

"Shut the fuck up," Jonny stammered. "Let me think."

"Poor singed Sadie will have nothing left to inherit now. Daddy banged up. Boyfriend missing in action. Not a penny to her name. If she ever needs a job, give Claire a shout. Cassie is niche. Some punters really don't care, do they?"

"Fuck you," Jonny roared. "I should just put a bullet in him now. Who gives a fuck?"

To Lorenzo's horror, Wellingham's finger flexed on the trigger. "Okay, okay." Lorenzo lowered the gun.

"Throw it over there."

Lorenzo did as he was told. The helicopter got steadily louder.

"Where were you heading?" Jonny snarled.

"A car's waiting for us," Lorenzo said. "In the car park over there."

"Then we move." Jonny shoved Harry. "You stay in front of us."

Lorenzo complied, his mind racing. Harry would not die tonight. He would not let that happen.

"Lift it," Jonny said, nodding to the loose bit of fencing.

Lorenzo pulled it as hard as he could. With the tip of his gun in Harry's neck, Jonny manoeuvred them under the gap.

"Be careful," Lorenzo said. "You kill him and I'll rip you from limb to limb."

"Big words," Jonny replied as he and Harry stood on the other side. "Now, you. Move."

Lorenzo crawled under the fence. He considered rushing Jonny when he got up, but the trigger would go off before he'd even made contact.

After they scrambled the embankment, a lone car sat in the car park. Lorenzo led Jonny and Harry over.

"And who do we have here?" Jonny said. "Little Liam. Get the fuck out."

A wide-eyed Liam got out of the car. "Jon. What the fuck are you doing?"

"Get over by him," Jonny shouted.

Liam followed his direction and moved next to Lorenzo. The poor lad was terrified.

"Now what, Wellingham?" Lorenzo asked. "Bit of a stand-off?"

"I'm taking the wheels. If you're lucky, the cops won't find you," Jonny sneered.

He moved over to the car. In one fluid motion, he threw Harry to the ground and jumped into the driver's seat. Before he could even close the door, Marco rose from the back and wrapped a belt around Jonny's neck. In a second, he had him pinned to the headrest.

In the confusion, Lorenzo saw his chance and dove for the gun. Jonny was so preoccupied with the shock, Lorenzo took it straight from his hand.

It could all end here. Lorenzo's finger tensed against the trigger. The temptation to blow Wellingham away gripped him from his feet up.

"Don't do it," Harry said. "You don't need to. We've done him over."

The chopper sounded again. It must be coming over their side to search for people. Lorenzo had to decide now what to do with Wellingham.

"Lorenzo, listen to me," Harry said. "I want to be free. Truly free. I'm begging you not to take that away."

Everything Jonny Wellingham had done to him rushed through his mind. Lying in that pool not knowing if he would survive. Going home to Rome with his tail between his legs. Jonny trying to kill anyone who he loved. Then turning his own nephew on him. Hate burnt through his system like lava.

This was the moment he'd spent most of his adult life working towards.

He glanced at Marco, who had a fierce scowl on his face. He would support Lorenzo no matter what. Yet Lorenzo could prove to Marco what a true leader did. What they had to do. They had to drown out all the noise and go with their gut instinct.

Lorenzo flinched at Harry's hand on his arm.

He fired the gun.

"No," Harry screamed.

Jonny writhed in pain. Lorenzo nodded to Marco who let him free. Jonny slid onto the floor from the gunshot wound Lorenzo had inflicted on his thigh. His trousers were already damp with blood. Walking forward, Lorenzo reached into his pocket and threw down a packet of drugs near to Jonny. "Just in case there's any confusion."

Calmly he got out his mobile phone and dialled nine-nine-nine.

"Police, please," Lorenzo said. When he was put through, he didn't even give the operator a chance to finish her speech. "Jonny Wellingham's garage was raided tonight. The police and his boys are still taking pot-shots at each other. Wellingham got away then got himself shot. You might want to send a copper and an ambulance to the soap factory car park."

Terminating the call, he turned to Harry who threw his arms around him. "I fucking love you."

"Help me," Marco said to Liam and they both pulled Jonny free of the car.

"You can't leave me," Jonny wailed. "Harry, after everything we've been through together. Finish the job, you cowardly fuck."

Instead, Lorenzo opened the car door for Harry. This was it. *The moment of no return.*

"Ignore him," Harry said. "Whatever he says, just ignore it."

"De Luca, I'll rat on the lot of you," Jonny screamed. "I'll arrange for you to have the cell next to me."

They all got in and slammed the doors.

"De Luca!" Jonny screamed.

Lorenzo waved out of the window at the once great Jonny Wellingham, lying on the floor, begging for mercy.

"Liam, get us out of here," Lorenzo said. "This place always did stink of absolute shit."

Liam put the car in gear and set off out of the car park. Once they were clear of any worries of the police picking them up, Marco let out a whoop. "Did you see his fucking face? When we just drove away. Oh my God, that was good."

"Nothing compared to his face when you popped up off the backseat," Lorenzo replied. "I think he pissed his pants right then and there."

"Were you tempted, Uncle?" Liam asked.

Lorenzo's heart warmed a little. It was the first time Liam had ever called him that and it made Lorenzo burst with pride. He would be proud to call Liam his nephew.

"I'd be a liar if I said I wasn't," Lorenzo said.

"What made you change your mind?" Harry asked.

"You."

The streetlights illuminated Harry's face. Lorenzo kissed him, long and hard. He didn't care who saw it anymore. He let his head fall onto Harry's shoulder. "Now we're free."

Harry took hold of his hand and kissed the back of it. "You weren't supposed to follow me."

"Well, it's a fucking good job I did. You'd either be banged up or dead now. What were you going to do?"

"I planned on triggering it and getting out of there without being caught. Seems Wellingham's lads aren't as shit as they look."

"They're also out of work," Lorenzo reminded. "Those that aren't getting banged up for shooting at the cops. What a bunch of twats."

They were coming into the city centre now. The big tower block where his product sat, the pubs and clubs that it would be sold in that coming weekend and the apartments where his girls would service those horny punters.

Once he would have found it exhilarating. Now he wanted to curl into bed and fall asleep in Harry's arms. *Fat chance of that.*

"Where to, Lorenzo?" Liam asked.

"The airport, of course. Claire is meeting us there with our things. I'm not wasting a plane ticket."

"Now?" Harry asked.

Lorenzo ran his hand along Harry's thick thigh. "You forced my hand, my love. You, me and Tommasso are booked on the next flight out of here."

"Tommasso?"

"His mother is waiting for him at Shaun and Enzo's. There won't be enough yoga in the world to calm her rage down. Tommasso is going to have a rough few days."

They all burst out laughing. Whether it was the adrenaline working its way through his system or the fact that he could start planning for a future in a way that most people took for granted, but Lorenzo couldn't stop.

"Fuck, it's over," Lorenzo said, raising his head and wiping his eyes.

He wanted to drink in Harry's face next to him.

"Or it's only just beginning," Harry said, following it up with a kiss.

They settled on the back seat again. The lights of the city centre fell behind them as they zoomed down the bypass. Lorenzo would probably never see this town again, but he had no desire to return. It was all for Marco and Liam now.

"I'm sorry to leave you in a mess, little one," he said. "As soon as we get home, I'll get a new delivery to you. I promise. Brooks will have to settle for that." He saw Marco and Liam exchange a look then giggle. Dread swept over him once more. "What is it?"

"Okay, I'll confess. While you were flapping in Claire's room, I woke Gab. He and Diego intercepted Jonny's vans. We're now the proud owners of two Ford Transits packed with goodies."

Lorenzo leant forward and hugged Marco. "Well done, little one. Well done."

"Thank you, Uncle."

Happiness washed over him. "There is nothing left for me to do now," Lorenzo said, taking hold of Harry's hand, "except to make up for the last fifteen years."

Harry reached into his pocket and got out the gold sovereign ring Lorenzo had returned to him that first day at Salford Quays. Gently, Harry slipped it onto his finger.

"It's where it belongs again," Harry said, kissing him on the cheek.

Lorenzo stared into his eyes. "And so am I."

Chapter Twenty-One

Six months later

Lorenzo dashed out onto the terrace. The sun beat down on it, making the tiles hot underneath his bare feet. His heart skipped the beat it always did every time he saw Harry, casually lying on a sun lounger. Lorenzo still couldn't believe that this was happening. Never in his wildest dreams had he thought his thirst for revenge would end like this.

However, he didn't have time to thank his lucky stars today. He had far too much on his mind for that. "What are you doing?" he asked.

"I'm taking a break," Harry said with a chuckle. "You've been barking orders since daybreak."

Perching on the wall, Lorenzo pouted. "Sorry for wanting everything to be perfect."

"It will be," Harry replied. "Stop fretting."

Lorenzo shook his head. "Could we sound any more like an old married couple?"

"Come on." Harry got to his feet. "I think I saw one of the lilies wilting in the guest bedroom."

They couldn't be. Lorenzo had only just checked them. Then he clocked the expression on Harry's face. "Oh, that was a joke? I think it best you leave those to me."

He allowed Harry to lead him into the villa, the marble floor cooling his feet. The place was nowhere near how he wanted it. Harry and he had found enjoyment in scouring local markets and shops for things to decorate their new home, yet he had grand plans of a possible extension and spa.

The lounge overlooked a valley of cypress trees with the spire of the village church just visible in the distance.

"It's a long way from Manchester. I hope they can get some rest."

"Well, limit the shop talk then," Harry said, plumping pillows on the couches. "Let him be your nephew and not your employee. He would love that, you know."

Lorenzo pulled him close. "I love you."

"I love you too."

They kissed, Harry's lips soft and inviting. Lorenzo had had a thousand of those kisses in that room and each one felt new. Parting his lips, Harry darted his tongue into Harry's mouth, the change of tempo unexpected yet not unwelcome.

Lorenzo ran his hands up Harry's arms, squeezing his biceps. He could feel Harry's hard-on through the thin shorts he had on.

"You can bloody stop that, as well."

They broke the kiss to see Shaun and Enzo stood in the doorway.

"Jesus Christ," Lorenzo said. "Is there no bloody privacy?"

Shaun burst into laughter which echoed through the high ceilings. "You said to come round for when they arrive. Is all this sex you're having addling your brain?"

"If it did that, you wouldn't be able to speak," Enzo fired back.

"Enzo," Shaun cried.

They stepped down into the lounge. In the six months that Lorenzo had got to know Shaun, he liked him more and more. The Moseley brothers had certainly made an impact on his family.

The buzzer rang through the house.

"They're here," Shaun said, clapping his hands together.

Harry darted to the intercom and pressed the button. Threats might be minimal nowadays, but they weren't impossible. Lorenzo had insisted on top-of-the-range security.

Glancing around the room, he checked that everything was perfect. His stomach did somersaults.

"Well, come on then," Harry said.

They all piled out of the door and onto the drive. A matte grey Alfa Romeo Giulia was coming up the drive. Lorenzo draped his arm around Harry. The day would be perfect.

Once the car had stopped, Marco, Liam, Claire, Federico and Gabriel all piled out.

"My babies," Lorenzo cried.

Marco dashed into his arms.

"Little one. It's good to see you." Lorenzo hugged him tight.

* * * *

The sunlight danced on the pool as Lorenzo raised a glass of champagne. The faces staring back at him were full of love. Well, except for the glowering Tommasso at the bottom of the table.

"Gentlemen and lady," Lorenzo began, nodding at Claire, "today is a big day for all of us. I'm glad that we can be together when we get the news. Even you, Tommasso."

Everyone turned and stared.

"It's more than you deserve," Marco sneered.

"Have no fear," Lorenzo said. "Tommasso is paying his dues."

Tommasso had been handed over to Shaun and Enzo. He did all the jobs in the yoga retreat that no one wanted to do.

"That's very true," Shaun said. "And to give him his credit, the toilets have never been cleaner. Have they, Enzo?"

"No," Enzo replied. "Just as well. The gardens probably need your magic touch soon."

Tommasso just scowled and looked away. The rest of the table sniggered. When they had presented Tommasso to his mother, she had already devised his punishment. Five years' hard labour in a family business where he could be kept an eye on. She was more than happy for that to be the one right under Lorenzo's nose.

As soon as they'd arrived, they'd changed into their pool wear and spent a wonderful hour acting up and laughing.

Now they sat around the glass dining table in the shadow of a cypress tree. The table groaned with food that Lorenzo and Harry had picked up in the local town—fruit and vegetables, cured meats and antipasti.

"Oh, this is the life," Claire said, leaning in her chair and letting the sun beat on her face. "I don't blame you for giving it all up."

"I wouldn't say that," Lorenzo said. "Marco still gives me a weekly call. Don't think I'm totally out of it."

"Are you happy?" Liam asked.

Lorenzo squeezed Harry's knee. "Like you wouldn't believe."

Federico's phone rang. He grabbed it. "It's the lawyer."

"Answer it then," Gabriel urged.

They all tensed. Liam grabbed Marco's hand. Lorenzo took Claire's in one hand and Harry's in the other.

"Hello?" Federico said.

They all studied him so intensely, desperately trying to read his face. Lorenzo cursed that Federico had always been a maddeningly good poker player.

"Okay. I'll let them know. Thank you."

He put the phone down on the table and looked at them all. Lorenzo cursed himself for teaching them all the value of a good dramatic moment. They were all as bad as he was.

"Spit it out. For fuck's sake," Claire said.

"Wellingham got twenty-two years."

The words hung in the air like fireworks about to go off. Then *boom*. Everyone started screaming and cheering and jumped up. Lorenzo flung his arms around Harry.

"Oh fuck," Lorenzo cried into his shoulder. "You fucking genius."

He kissed him hard on the lips before breaking away to take hugs from everyone. All except Tommasso who just sat there as if nothing was happening.

When the jubilation died down. Lorenzo grabbed his glass. "Now we drink to two friends who can't be here with us because of that piece of shit. May their faces haunt his fucking dreams."

"May their faces haunt his fucking dreams," everyone repeated.

They drank deeply from the flutes. Jonny had inflicted wounds that would eventually scab over but never truly go. That was the name of the game. Lorenzo had tried to forget the things he had done in his life. They never truly left him. He would wake in the night with a face or a memory. He had Harry's arms to make him feel still again. Wellingham had nothing.

"And what about Deano?" Liam asked.

"Fifteen," Federico said. "The other lads got ten each."

Liam smiled at Harry. "Poor old Deano, eh?"

"Fuck Deano," Harry replied. "That nasty little bastard deserves it."

Lorenzo clapped his hands together. "Okay, this calls for a celebration of global magnitude. Tonight, we'll go into town in our best clothes. I want to wake up tomorrow morning feeling the worst I've ever done in my life."

They all cheered.

* * * *

The next morning saw Lorenzo's wishes come true, with the early morning sun blazing through the flimsy curtains.

He lay for a second trying to gauge just how bad the hangover was going to be. His mind strayed to the night before. It had been joyous to have everyone here.

Spending time with Liam and Marco always made his heart swell. It was no secret Marco was his favourite. That he had found someone who saw exactly what Lorenzo did made him want to weep with happiness.

Since they'd arrived at the villa, he had really got to know Shaun. Once again it was a perfect love match between him and Enzo. Shaun's bubbly personality was calmed by Enzo's thoughtful disposition.

It gave Lorenzo pride to think he had been a big part in these young men finding love.

The breeze from the open window shifted the curtain and he felt as though the sun's rays were boring deep into his brain.

"When we do this room, we're getting fucking blackout blinds," he grumbled.

"Feeling rough?" Harry asked.

That was an understatement. Lorenzo's mouth was as arid as the Sahara and a pneumatic drill seemed to be going off in his head. He desperately needed water yet lacked the energy to raise his head.

"I'm getting too old for this," Lorenzo complained.

"I did try to tell you that but no, you had to have another sambuca."

His stomach gurgled in response. Lorenzo tried to ignore the urge to throw up. Why did he always have to prove a point?

"At least I wasn't sick." He chuckled as the memory of poor Marco hanging out of the taxi popped into his head. "Once again, little one costs me a fortune."

Harry sniggered and buried his nose into Lorenzo's hair. They snuggled, enjoying the moment of calm after the madness of the day before.

"It feels good, doesn't it?" Harry said. "Waking up truly free. I really thought his lawyer would come up with something and get him a reduced sentence."

Lorenzo squeezed Harry's hand. "They've wanted that slimeball for years. Once they trapped him, he was fucked."

"Once we trapped him, you mean," Harry replied.

Lorenzo turned over so he faced Harry. He ignored the wave of nausea because he wanted to look into his lover's eyes. "Will you marry me?"

Harry's eyes widened. "What?"

"You heard. You once wrote a note saying you couldn't trust me. Now I'm saying that isn't true. You can trust me with anything and I think it needs saying to the world. Marry me, Harry. Please."

Harry stared at him. "Harry de Luca? I quite like it."

"Is that a yes?"

"Of course it's a yes, you idiot. I would love to marry you."

His heart was fit to burst. Marrying Harry had been preying on his mind ever since they'd arrived in Tuscany. Once Jonny had been sentenced and they were finally rid of him, Lorenzo had told himself he would ask.

Kissing Harry hard, he worried he couldn't take this level of happiness. It was heady and exhilarating.

He sat up and pulled the sovereign ring off. Harry gave him his hand and he slipped it onto Harry's ring finger.

"We're going to have to buy another one of those." Harry chuckled. "It flits between us like a ping pong ball."

Lorenzo squeezed his hand. "I don't mind sharing with you, Mr de Luca."

"Come here," Harry said. "Let me try you on for size."

Lorenzo fell into his arms. "You've tried me on a few times now, my love."

"Ah yes, as a lover. Now you're a fiancé. That's a whole different ballgame."

The word set bubbles of happiness fizzing around Lorenzo's system. "And how do I fit?"

"Like a glove."

Their lives were laid before them now. Decades of contentment as they grew old together. The fifteen years apart would fade into obscurity, pushed aside by more memories than they knew what to do with.

For the first time in his adult life, Lorenzo knew he had come home.

Want to see more from this author? Here's a taster for you to enjoy!

Village Affairs: The Rule of Three
Kristian Parker

Excerpt

Disco music blasted from the float passing by, and the crowds jamming the pavements dancing and waving in the spring sunshine cheered as a drag queen belted out *Holding Out For A Hero* at the top of her lungs.

A six-foot-tall man dressed as Wonder Woman threw a condom directly at Ed Cropper It ricocheted off his head and fell straight into his beer.

"Lo siento," 'she' cried and blew him a kiss.

She disappeared into the crowd, soon to be replaced by a marching band in stockings and suspenders. The parade waited for no one.

Ed fished the rogue item out of his beer and slid it into his shirt pocket.

James Durkin wrapped his arm around his shoulder. "Could you be any more Yorkshire? Waste not, want not?" he asked, laughing.

Ed leant into the hug, the throng of sweaty bodies pushing them together and the overwhelming smell of poppers permeating through the crowd. It only ever gave him a headache. He wondered what the hell anyone was doing sniffing them in the glaring Spanish sun.

"*Ah, guapo, guapo*," shouted another drag queen, resplendent as Ursula from *The Little Mermaid*. She made a beeline for Ed and James, kissing them both on the cheeks before plunging their faces into her bosom.

They gasped as they came up for air and she blew kisses.

"It's bloody *mental* this year." James grinned.

The parade tailed off, leaving the crowd to disperse. Every bar had rainbow flags and cheap shots, but several years' experience had taught Ed that Maspalomas Pride was a marathon, not a sprint...although the glint in James' eye said he'd happily hit the booze.

"Right. Come on, you," Ed said. "Let's get some supplies and have a disco nap. Keep your strength up."

"Spoilsport," James replied.

They broke off from the crowd and wandered down an alley towards the apartment they'd rented. It was so close to everything that they'd snapped it up the second they'd come home last year.

James put his shirt on and walked with a spring in his step. Ed caught sight of them both in a boutique window. The drag queen had been right. They did make a handsome couple. Six-foot-three James had piercing blue eyes, a receding hairline that he shaved and lightly tan skin. Ed, on the other hand, had long dark curls, a beard and an even deeper tan from working outdoors most of his life.

Once inside, the cool relief in the supermarket made Ed gasp. It had been so hot in the middle of that crowd. James stood by the huge fan, letting his shirt billow behind him.

"What are you like?" Ed chuckled, picking up a basket and starting to think about what they needed.

James followed him up the aisle. Ed picked up some juice and bits to snack on. He absolutely refused to turn the cooker on in the apartment, but they had to survive, didn't they? He turned and saw James holding up eggs, bread and cheese.

"Please can I have your French toast for breakfast?" James asked with his pathetic puppy-dog face.

Ed sighed. "Not a chance, buster. You can take me out for French toast."

James slowly dropped the items in the basket. "But no one makes it like you do. You're the best French toast chef this side of Paris."

Ed couldn't resist those eyes. "Fine, seeing as it's you."

"Thank you, Eduardo," James said with a wink. "I'll make it worth your while."

It made Ed cross when James called him that and he bloody knew it. "Will you now?"

"Definitely."

"Then you've definitely got a deal."

Ed went to kiss him but leapt like a scalded cat as James put a hand on his chest and pushed him away.

"What are you doing?" James whispered, checking around the deserted aisle to see if anyone had seen them.

Ed's chest still stung from where James' fingertips had rejected him. "Nothing." He continued walking up the aisle but could sense James wasn't following him and spun round. James had that confused face he used to pull in primary school when asked a particularly difficult question. Ed had found it adorable then and he still did.

"What is the matter with you?" James asked calmly.

It drove Ed mad that he never seemed to lose his cool. Ed threw the basket down on the floor with a clatter. "Ten minutes ago, you were happy to kiss a drag queen and take your shirt off. Now you push me away?"

James snatched up the basket. "Are we having an argument in the fucking shampoo aisle?"

"No, James. We couldn't do that because someone might hear us," Ed replied and stormed past him and out of the shop.

Tears were threatening to escape as he dashed across the busy street and down another alley which led to their apartment. He had the key and let himself into the dusty stairway where they'd kissed on nearly every step after they'd got home the night before.

Today he stomped up each one, desperately trying to leave his anger on them but only feeling more uptight the higher he climbed. By the time he got inside, the tears had gone and he paced the apartment. James would be here any minute and Ed really didn't want to ruin the holiday by having a row.

He grabbed a beer from the fridge and walked out onto the balcony. The dull thud of the dance music from the huge party a stone's throw away swept across the rooftops. Gaggles of men would be dancing in each other's arms. Not afraid of anything.

Ed had always known he was attracted to men, but there had only ever been one he'd truly wanted. The man charging across the street below with a bag of shopping. He took a long slug of the cold beer and waited for the intercom to sound. It didn't take long before the harsh buzz filled the room. With a sigh, he wandered over.

"Are you going to let me in?" James' crackly voice questioned him.

Ed pushed the button and replaced the receiver. As a couple, they weren't the type to be constantly arguing and making up. They achieved this mainly as Ed did everything he could to keep the peace. He hated confrontation. It upset him and he'd replay it over and over, long after James had forgotten about it.

But he'd started this one and now James' footsteps echoed on the stairs. He would soon be wanting answers and Ed just wasn't ready to have the conversation he'd been practising for a while now. He went out onto the balcony again. James had a habit of filling a room and could be totally overpowering. Ed had always been more the type to shrink and marvel at how James could find a way to talk to anyone.

James came through the wooden panelled door and threw the shopping bag down onto the glass dining table. "Are you going to talk to me?" he asked, joining Ed on the balcony. He took his beer from his hand and had a swig.

Ed got up and padded inside. James' eyes bored into him as he got another drink from the buzzing fridge. It annoyed him that James had left the door open. He worried about mosquitos getting in, but the look on James' face hadn't lessened any and he thought it best to leave it for now.

"I'm still waiting, Ed."

Ed went back outside and sat on the rickety old chair. "Why couldn't you kiss me?" he asked eventually.

"You know why," James said, leaning against the railing. "What if someone sees us?"

Ed threw his hands up in the air. "We're miles away from anyone we know. And who cares if they do?"

"It's just not my thing. You know it isn't."

But what if it's mine? Ed couldn't face carrying on this conversation. They had dinner plans for the evening and he had no intention of eating with a cloud hanging over them. "Fine, whatever. I'm sorry I caused a scene. It just hurt me, you know?"

He got up to put the shopping away. James grabbed hold of his arm and drew him inward, wrapping his arms around his shoulders. Ed could smell the citrussy aftershave James had bought at the airport. It worked well on him, and he allowed himself to be drawn into a hug.

"You daft bugger. I love you no matter what. I wouldn't do anything to hurt you and I'd bloody kill anyone who did."

Feeling the strong arms resting on his shoulders made everything all right again. It always had.

"Come here," James said with a glint in his eye.

He moved Ed so he faced out to the whole of Maspalomas and stood behind him, lifting his arms like Leo did to Kate in *Titanic*.

"I bloody love this man," James shouted, almost deafening Ed in the process. "I always have and I always will."

A few people down below cheered. James spun him around and planted his lips on his. "There you go. Happy now?"

With that, he went inside and busied himself putting the shopping away. Ed watched him, marvelling at how pleased with himself James seemed. But the nagging doubt inside Ed still gnawed away at him. James had done it to keep him sweet, not because he wanted to. This secret love affair seemed to be all James wanted. A week in the sunshine every year then sneaking around the village they lived in for the rest of it.

Ed sighed and tried to shake the feeling that had been creeping into his mind for months.

The feeling that this…wasn't enough for him anymore.

About the Author

I have written for as long as I could write. In fact, before, when I would dictate to my auntie. I love to read, and I love to create worlds and characters.

I live in the English countryside. When I'm not writing, I like to get out there and think through the next scenario I'm going to throw my characters into.

Inspiration can be found anywhere, on a train, in a restaurant or in an office. I am always in search of the next character to find love in one of my stories. In a world of apps and online dating, it is important to remember love can be found when you least expect it.

Kristian loves to hear from readers. You can find his contact information, website details and author profile page at https://www.pride-publishing.com

PUBLISHING

Sign up for our newsletter and find out about all our romance book releases, eBook sales and promotions, sneak peeks and FREE romance books!